THIS WORLD OF FARMERS

RAVI NAMBIAR

WRITERS' READERS
AN IMPRINT OF BOOKSTHAKAM PUBLISHERS

Published by Writers' Readers, an imprint of Booksthakam Publishers

Booksthakam India, 4B Muthoot Rainbow, AKG Nagar, Peroorkada
Thiruvananthapuram, Kerala 695005, India

info@booksthakam.com
www.booksthakam.com

THIS WORLD OF FARMERS

A Booksthakam Book / published by arrangement with the author

ISBN-13: 978-93-94378-21-6

To all the fellow 'farmers' of this world.

CONTENTS

CHAPTER ONE

With a lumbering portrait of a beautiful South Indian actress painted on its side panel, the bus stood rather haughtily at the town junction, waiting for the passengers impatiently. The impatience was evident in the intermittent acceleration of the engine by the driver. The vendors at the intersection noisily prepared their snacks, beating the hot pans occasionally with their spatulas, inviting customers. A few people stood at the counters awaiting their dinner while others ate hurriedly, focusing intently on their plates. A chemist rolled down the metal shutter of his shop with a clang. He checked and double-checked the brass lock by tugging at it several times. A bakery owner pushed his extended display glass counter inside his small shop to pull down the rolling shutter. Everyone was winding up, returning home after a long day.

Just as Angad boarded the bus; the driver zoomed off, veering through the thinning late evening crowd. Breathing heavily, Angad balanced himself in the wobbling bus. He tossed himself into a plush aisle chair. In a quick flash from the passing street light, Angad managed to get a fleeting glimpse of the long-bearded elderly man next to him, cocooned with his legs folded in the seat and his eyes wide open.

This last-minute travel was unexpected and annoying. Tucking a few necessities into his backpack, Angad had announced his expedition to his mother; making it out to be just another of his usual business trips. Hurriedly, he packed his luggage as his mother followed him around; badgering him with questions about this sudden trip.

For Angad, this terrible development early in the morning was too much to handle. He was running away from his hometown, his job at the bank and everything around him. It had all begun to frighten him.

Once aboard the bus, Angad saw how the passengers lived in a world of their own. While some breathed heavily, some whistle-snored, others moved restlessly; thoughts racing through their minds. Consciously or unconsciously, they all had managed to create a world of beliefs. Suddenly, a passenger from the last row groaned, causing a few to grumble. "I am too in an abstract world, stuck on what happened this morning;" Angad thought to himself. He folded his legs on the uncomfortable seat, trying to catch some sleep. His co-traveller; an elderly man, was disturbed by Angad's frequent movements and he coughed to express his displeasure. How a cough can speak one's mind!

As the world outside slept, Angad took a look at himself. He looked at his hands, his fingers and his chewed-out nails. As if in a reverie, he withdrew physically and left to look for the 'real' Angad, who was nowhere to be found. The world is not outside. It is inside; it's inside each individual! As the bus made its way; Angad felt a sense of relief, albeit temporarily. A few hours later, his co-passenger started snoring. He pushed the glass window open, trying to read the roadside billboards to find out where he reached. The sudden gust of wind from the window was met with loud, angry comments from his co-travellers. He seemed upset about something. "What would have made him leave his wife, children, or even grandchildren?" The light from the passing streetlights reflected on his stained teeth and uneven grey beard.

Suddenly, the man looked out of the window and asked the driver to stop. He had reached his destination. The driver turned on the aisle lights as the older man carried his small bag in one hand while the other hand was busy, keeping his loose trousers from sliding. He jumped out of the bus and disappeared into the darkness of the night suspiciously. "Like me, the world he carried on his head was too heavy," Angad thought to himself.

The bus hurried along; it had to reach its destination. The conductor yelled: "Hospital Street! Hospital Street -- Anyone?" Angad hastened off the bus, stubbing his toe against a stone on the pavement.

An old concrete signboard announced: 'Hospital Street.' Music wafted in with the morning breeze making the air lighter. Birds joined in the symphony, celebrating the birth of another day!

Angad checked the time, it was almost six. It was an inapt time to call Raghu. Instead, he would try to find Raghu's home. So, he set out in search of the third floor of house number thirteen in the second cross. Angad recalled that Raghu had told him that the apartment was diagonally opposite a hospital run by monks. Angad placed the backpack on the causeway. He saw a tea vendor serving piping hot tea with South Indian breakfast below a rusted metal board stating, 'Hotel Anand Bhavan.' The vendor gingerly strained and poured the scalding hot tea into glasses laid out on the counter.

The city was no stranger. Angad had visited here a few years ago and thought it was a conservative place. It had changed since then. Huge glass-front buildings had come up, with many engineers now earning their bread and butter here; writing codes for the world and turning the place into a dream destination for other aspiring engineers and job seekers. He walked briskly, counting the streets and buildings.

When he reached Raghu's room, Raghu was surprised at his unannounced arrival. He sat in his chair, scratching his shiny pate; wondering about the reason behind Angad's sudden visit. Angad threw his bag in a corner and sat at the edge of the metal cot that made a sudden screeching noise. Raghunandan – Angad loved the name! Whenever he said this name, he felt its radiance all around it. Raghu worked as an auditor for the Accountant General's office in the city. Scrutinizing expense vouchers was the love of his life. He loved it more than anything else. Touring various district headquarters, he hunted for forged expenditures and other misdemeanours of government officials. His frequent trips meant leaving his wife in Mysore and living the life of a bachelor.

Angad had first met Raghu while in college. He had a thick bush of hair and was rather timid. Raghu remained a calm, quiet and polite person. He spoke little and never judged people. He was always unbothered no matter what happened around him. So, he wasn't even concerned about why Angad had arrived without a word of warning. Still, seeing an upset Angad, Raghu questioned him.

Raghu's jaws dropped when Angad gave him the reason for his unannounced visit. Angad was looking for a hideout – a refuge – a place to hide himself indefinitely. Raghu was more than happy to have the company of an old classmate when he would return home from his frequent trips.

Angad stepped out into the balcony for a view of the majestic Hospital Street lined with trees. The canopy loomed over the street, standing tall in eternal peace. They seemed to sympathise with men and women passing below, striving for material wealth, despite knowing that nothing would remain forever.

Raghu warned Angad not to leave the balcony door open. There were a lot of monkeys around. "They are aggressive and come in packs to pick anything that pleases them," he explained. Hotel Anand Bhavan was also partially visible from the balcony. It seemed as if the entire neighbourhood was enveloped in the aroma of freshly made *sambar* from the restaurant.

Angad lingered on, watching people below on the streets. He seemed to be lost in his own world when Raghu broke his reverie, saying, "One can easily lose track of time if one keeps looking at this busy street." Raghu always spoke like a true accountant, relating anything to reconciliation and final balancing. The dedicated auditor of funds left for the office, having groomed himself in front of an antique, stained, wooden framed mirror placed in the living room. In his official garb, Raghu looked cut out for the job. The stained mirror had different coloured *bindis* stuck on its corner, like placards of his wife's visits, who occasionally spent a few days in the apartment, especially after a tiff with her mother-in-law.

The patio opened up to the world: a branch of blossoming Gulmohar invading a portion of the government housing scheme building. The elevated spot offered a broader view. A busy bus shelter next to the hospital that lent the name to the street, a temple, Ananda Bhavan, a few business establishments, retail outlets and an office of some defence establishment on the other side.

Soon, Angad saw Raghu standing near the bus shelter holding a black leather bag. A bus stopped and scooped some of the anxiously waiting officegoers, including him. At a distance from the bus stop, neatly dressed schoolchildren played under the watchful eyes of their parents while they waited for their school buses.

"My mind is like a motor, it thinks continuously," Angad thought. "It never stops, not even in my sleep. It's the same with all creatures. All beings think, ponder; feel with a mind they have no control over," he brooded. He leaned over the parapet to get a clearer view; he was getting addicted to watching people already. He noticed a giant anthill in the middle of the footpath sprinkled with vermillion and garlanded with a long string of flowers. "Do beliefs make the world go on?" he pondered.

A few feet away, a cobbler had encroached the footpath by making a make-shift shop of steel which was the size of an extra-large carton. A faded picture of Dr Ambedkar adorned the blue-painted, dented metal background. The old cobbler sat behind a heap of footwear, meticulously refurbishing them one after the other. A clay pot seller sat near him with hundreds of pots of different shapes and sizes stacked on the pavement; some looked old and dusty, probably stacked there for years seasoned by nature. The vegetation and the earthen pots merged amiably, making it look like a fine work of art.

Angad continued to scan the world on the Hospital Street. A vegetable hawker announced his entry onto the scene. The cart displayed fresh vegetables of every size and colour. He maintained a slow and steady pace on his unwieldy cart with its faulty wheel alignment. He yelled out the names of the vegetables on his cart, audible yet not clear. It seemed he did not care if potential buyers understood what he offered. He just wanted to ensure that the residents in his vicinity knew that their regular vegetable vendor had arrived.

A playful monkey showed up on one of the lower branches touching the balcony, prompting Angad to maintain a safe distance. Without warning, it suddenly jumped and swung from branch to branch disappearing into the thick foliage. The vegetable vendor halted his cart to attend to his regular clients who chatted with each other on trivial matters. The vendor lifted a large musk melon; cut it skilfully, weighed it and handed it to the woman waiting for it. He kept talking to them, praising the quality and freshness of his vegetables. He informed everyone about how he had sourced it from the market in the wee hours of the morning. The hawker frequently broke into his typical announcement, in the middle of selling vegetables: it was a listing of all vegetables on the earth, never mind whether he had them or not. That did not matter at all.

CHAPTER TWO

Even behind the long grey moustache, Narendra Prasad was unable to hide his discomfort as Angad entered the portico of his house. Narendra flashed a smile but he was uneasy in his friend's presence. In the past fortnight, Angad had called him numerous times, but all his calls went unanswered, which left Angad with no choice but to pay him a visit.

An old jeep and a white Maruti car were parked, amongst farm equipment; tools and broken-down tractors. Heaps of hay and rice hulls festooned the yard. The double-storey house with a red-tiled roof, even though old and unkempt, stood out royally among other homes in the vicinity. Any stranger would get the impression that the house belonged to a wealthy family. One portion of the house had been expanded to make a thatched cow shelter, large enough to accommodate half a dozen jersey cows; they seemed to enjoy chewing the cud with froth oozing out from their mouths.

Narendra Prasad's finances were a far cry from all the visible abundance. The man was neck-deep in debt. Angad had failed to recover the bank's money loaned to him. Narendra Prasad insisted that Angad's jeep, with a large bank logo, be parked inside the compound wall. He wanted to hide it from the prying eyes of the people in his locality. Angad obliged.

As a probationer in a national bank, Angad had opted to work in the agriculture segment. He had thought that it would be fun to work in rural areas, away from the hustle and bustle of the city and had dreamt of visiting the countryside, meeting farmers, spending quality time with them and enjoying green pastures. Angad had nurtured dreams for his village assignments. However, he soon realised that life in rural areas was not as lush green as he had thought, for every farmer had a dark story -- a story of account books that would not balance. Even in good times of a bumper crop, expenses always ended up outweighing income.

Some of the farmers he met had never maintained accounts of their expenditures. There seemed to be no cap on spending; no assumption on the minimum possible income, and they blindly kept farm activities going by borrowing beyond their capacities to pay off the loans. Farming for them was more like a ritual. For instance, Vasu, who farmed ginger, belonged to the same village as Prasad. But even after decades, the basics of farming seemed to have eluded him, and he had learnt nothing. Gullible middlemen still managed to con him, as his financial condition continued to deteriorate with every passing harvest. His debts surged despite bumper crops and a good price.

Ramana, the dealer of agricultural inputs; who had his store at the town crossroad, had been Vasu's friend from childhood. One would find him in white trousers and a matching shirt, flashing a heavy gold bracelet and platinum rings studded with precious stones. Naturally, an intimidated Vasu could not ask him questions. When Vasu went to Ramana to discuss any trivial issue about his farm, Ramana would listen carefully. Then, pulling out a piece of paper from a pad printed with pictures of insecticides, he would scribble the names of a few items and pass it to a waiting assistant who would get busy collecting the listed items. Ramana would also give Vasu some directions on how to use the insecticide. Vasu never questioned the instructions or the products. Before Vasu could reach his farm with a bagful of bottles and packets that he never knew how to use, Ramana would have jotted down the dues in his account book. The trouble was that the village had so many other Vasus.

Prasad and his family bent over backwards to be hospitable. They served snacks and tea to Angad, treating him like a guest. Prasad yelled at a labourer and gave him instructions on ploughing and watering, to which the tanned worker listened patiently. A volley of questions followed that Prasad answered patiently and concluded by saying, "I'll come a little later." Assured by the promise, the worker broke into a smile that revealed his stained teeth, leaving some tools from the yard. Others did menial jobs in the front yard and one of them walked the cattle out through the gate to graze. A lone young calf left behind in the shelter mooed to express its restlessness after the other cows had left.

Fifteen minutes later, Angad screwed up the courage to deal with the matter at hand. He always found it uncomfortable to ask for money, as he had had an earful from the branch manager. He had a miserable track record in the recovery of loans given out to farmers. Narendra Prasad guided Angad away from his family. He did not want to be shamed before them because they didn't know of his precarious financial condition. A few crows were fluttering around the courtyard as they searched for grubs in the heap of cow dung. The stink of cow dung and urine made Angad nauseous.

Once they were at a safe distance from the house, Prasad spoke softly, "Just fifteen more days! I will clear fifty per cent of the balance. The chillies are almost ready for harvest. I have also asked for some money from a businessman friend of mine in Bangalore." His husky voice tried to retain whatever little was left of his self-esteem. He did not want a soul to hear that their supposedly 'wealthy' landlord was pleading with a bank official for an extension on a loan. Angad sensed that Prasad wanted to see him on his way as fast as possible.

Angad had been instructed by the senior manager of the recovery division to give a curt notice to defaulters. Legal action would have to be initiated against the steadily growing number of defaulters. However, after hearing the plight of most farmers, Angad was always in a dilemma; it was difficult for him to initiate any proceedings against the defaulters.

It never ceased to amaze Angad how farmers would spend borrowed money on the most irrelevant things; they failed to maintain a basic account book, keep a tab on spending, and spent more than they could possibly earn. The harvested crop was never sold at proper prices because they could not hold on to the stock for long periods in order to get higher prices. Usually, farmers would sell under duress to middlemen. Trapped in this quagmire, Angad realised that he was not cut out for this job.

Vasu's wedding ring had been pledged at the pawnbroker Ramlal & Co. The same Ramlal, who wore flashy gold-rimmed spectacles hooked to a red string as he sat behind a red cloth-bound account book placed on top of a wooden box. That book had each borrower's history, and he kept the accounts that were easily traceable—certainly faster than any computer. When someone seeking a loan came to pledge a gold ornament, or brass or copper vessel; his wife who moved around the shop covered from head to toe in her fluorescent saree would inspect each item before giving her nod for the approval of the loan. Once that was done, quietly she would slink off into the house.

Ramlal's face betrayed no emotion. He was inscrutable. Those who borrowed brought collaterals. They had to wait forever to get any response from him. It could be a simple 'yes' or 'no' with a shake of the head. Over the years, Ramlal had gathered a large collection of wedding rings, *mangal-sutras*, bell metal spouted pitchers, and copper and brass kitchenware awaiting redemption by their rightful owners living in the village. What bothered Angad was the fact that people living in the villages could not adapt to change. To him, it seemed that they did not care whether their produce could fetch them good money. They carried on with their outdated ways and it was no surprise that the crafty agents or middlemen, all got together to trap them. Of course, there was a vast reservoir of good agricultural practices, but they knew little about managing money. Unless they came together to form a united front, there was no redemption and no easy way out for the farmers.

Many a time, Angad had pleaded with the bank's top brass to train farmers about the intricacies of basic finance. He felt that it could easily be incorporated into rural finance schemes but all his pleas seemed to fall on deaf ears. They were unmoved. In one such meeting held to discuss the increasing challenges faced in loan recovery, he had argued that farmers should be taught how to manage money. The regional manager made Angad a laughing stock by mocking him in the presence of all. For bankers, profit was the name of the game. After all, business was far more important to them and not the welfare of the farmers, the bank manager insisted.

For Anand Shetty, the regional manager with the receding hairline, it was a matter of routine to turn down any suggestions. He conducted many meetings to address the problems of loan recovery but would only yell at the officers. He adjourned meetings and simply refused to take a final call. Obviously, Angad realised that no one really cared about the farmers.

Ever since he joined the bank, he realised that he had no financial expertise just like his clients and that he was doing something he never wanted to do. Yet there he was, surrounded by people who always thought, ate and talked about money.

Returning to his jeep, Angad turned around to see Prasad at the entrance with his wife and daughters. They had no inkling of the deep anguish that Prasad was in. With a perplexed mind, he found it hard to drive over the pothole-ridden panchayat road. Every day, the people he met as a loan officer were always struggling to make ends meet. The very thought that he would be surrounded by countless farmers, caught in the middle of financial whirlwinds, worried him no end.

Meanwhile, the bank's head office had issued a long list of defaulting customers whose properties were to be confiscated using special powers. A copy of this list was on Angad's table too. Narendra Prasad's name was on top of the list because his dues were long outstanding and such action by the bank was inevitable. He had broken deadline after deadline and his outstanding loan, including compounding interest over the years, was around twelve lakhs. The figure was so high that it was impossible for him to make even a partial payment or enough to stall the confiscation proceedings.

Angad dialled Prasad out of impulse. As usual, Prasad did not respond to the call. He wanted to tell him that the bank was planning to foreclose after serving him a notice. But his calls over the next week remained unanswered. When he went to meet Prasad at his house, as expected the man was ashamed and listed out various reasons for not repaying. He began to open a box of promises to make payment the following week. Prasad's wife served hot tea and savouries. His children in their teens moved around the veranda. They ran and jumped amidst the sacks of grains and heaps of dry straw. They were warned by their doting father not to roll down the straw. But who would listen?

The permeating smell was intoxicating the surroundings: the straw, cow dung, cow urine, and freshly dug soil had a heady smell. Prasad's unorganised way of handling finance is reflected in the way he left things cluttered around him. Prasad just laughed when he was told that the bank had already sent a notice through the post and that he would be receiving it soon. Angad felt helpless at Prasad's indifferent attitude to such a serious matter. He reminded Prasad that he had pledged his house to the bank and that the bank could confiscate it. "What would you do if the bank takes such an extreme step?" Prasad was not moved. He evaded an answer, rolling his pointed, long moustache. Angad was sick to the pit of his stomach on the drive back, cursing his fate for dealing with people who took such serious issues so lightly. "The man would only learn his lesson when the bank takes over his property," he thought to himself. Desperately manoeuvring around large boulders on the road, he thought for a moment that maybe these people deserve to be penalised for taking developments so casually.

A few days later, when the notice arrived from the bank's advocate, Prasad panicked and called Angad in a quivering voice, whimpering over the phone. This was a whole new Prasad, who was worried about his wife and suddenly seemed concerned about his children. Angad sympathised with him, sad at the turn of events. However, there was little he could do and was helpless as he reminded Prasad of his warning. Angad knew that there was no use raking up the past. To the repeated requests of Prasad to delay the process, Angad said that he would try to help him, but he was not sure what exactly he could do at that point. Angad was unsure if he would gather the courage to talk to his seniors at the bank. They were already annoyed with his poor recovery performance. By now, a sentimental Angad knew that recovering money from such financially weak farmers was something he couldn't do. He calmed Prasad before the telephone conversation was over as he had a special liking for Prasad and his family. Though the house and its surroundings were a constant mess, Angad liked it. While the stink of cow dung and urine inebriated him, the smell of fresh soil gave him a high. It was perhaps the first time Prasad had tried to contact Angad on his own. Why only Prasad? Most people would have done the same under the given circumstances.

He was sure that Prasad would lose the only property that was in his name and that he would have to leave the house with his wife and two children. Where would they go? How would he take care of his family who never knew their actual financial status? Would they be able to cope with the new situation? Where would the children giggle and play around? Would they be able to pay their school fees and continue their studies? A proud Prasad would have to hang his head in shame. The people in the village would gossip. Would he be able to face it? The thoughts froze Angad.

He got up from the bed and drank a few gulps

of water from the bottle next to his bed. He went to the window and looked out. The darkness outside concealed more than it revealed. He was restless and worried about Prasad's family. Maybe the family could move in with a close relative? Would Prasad feel comfortable in someone's home? Maybe not! Prasad would only find comfort in his home, in his carved wooden chair, where he would twirl and twist his oiled moustache. Angad fell asleep thinking of ways to help Prasad.

The next morning, Angad was ready to request his superiors to extend some more time for the repayment. However, he was not sure that Prasad would manage to get the money together even with the extended duration. Two days passed without any development. Prasad would often call Angad over the phone to seek an extension of loan repayment. Each time, his voice turned more panic-stricken and anxious.

A helpless Angad pacified Prasad, that he would do something even though he was unsure of what exactly he would do. Despite his best efforts, nothing happened in Prasad's favour, since even the notice period to repay the loan was over.

Early morning, Angad headed towards Prasad's village. He thought that he would surprise Prasad in the morning with a temporary solution to his problems; he had managed a personal loan of two lakh rupees from the bank to help Prasad. He had made the payment to the bank on behalf of Prasad. Therefore, the bank had temporarily suspended the legal proceedings. It was his mother's suggestion to help the family after hearing about their plight. Upon hearing this, she was more worried about Prasad's wife and children. She was curious to know more about them. His father was unaware of the happenings. Had he been consulted, he would have never supported the idea of assisting a man who had taken a loan from the employer's bank -- "How can a loan recovery officer help every farmer this way?"

Angad was happy and satisfied that he was able to help his client. He thought Prasad would be delighted to hear about these developments. All that Prasad expected was to get more time from the bank to repay the loan, but this temporary relief in the form of financial support would come as a breath of fresh air. He imagined how Prasad would react to the payment receipt and how he would thank Angad profusely. His wife would offer him a cup of piping hot tea accompanied by snacks cooked in pure ghee. His children would be running around the heap of hay or braiding their hair to leave for school. They would be grateful to him for his generosity. The joyous mood helped make the otherwise bumpy ride a bit smoother. Angad no longer cursed the boulders scattered on the road or the endless potholes. Angad was on a ride to win the hearts of those he had learnt to love.

CHAPTER THREE

A grotesque spider continued in its efforts to weave a delicate web at the corner of the smoked ceiling. It pulled the silken threads with a rhythm, engrossed in building a delicate trap. A web of deep remorse trapped Angad. He saw no escape. The spider worked relentlessly. Lying down, Angad was mesmerised by every single movement of the spider. Prasad too had woven a web and trapped himself in it. A trap from which he could never come out.

The day had dawned. The hay stacked in heaps was moist with morning mist. The smell of the damp grass filled the air. The cows tied to stumps moved around restlessly, with a few black crows settled on their back. The daily labourers had not turned up at work. The main wooden door remained locked. A few hens shuttled about with their heads tilted, looking for grains. A stray dog wandered around. It appeared as if Prasad and his family were not home but the door was unlocked.

Angad took out his phone and called Prasad a few times. The calls remained unanswered. Angad was excited to inform Prasad and show him the receipt that he had made a part of the payment and bought Prasad some more time to repay the balance. Angad strolled around the front yard hoping that Prasad would turn up. Had he gone to the nearby temple? Had he gone off to the field? But where are his wife and children? Angad made himself at home and sat down on the century-old wooden chair on the veranda amidst the strong stench of cow dung and urine as he waited for Prasad to appear.

A few photographs adorned the stained walls, framed with thick wooden borders. Some images had lost their original colour, and there were dark stains too. The latest one was of Narendra Prasad sporting his signature moustache. He looked sharp and royal in the photograph. It resembled those of kings and emperors in the old history textbooks in school. The cows went around the stumps they were tied to and mooed impatiently, looking at the house. The stray, the hens and a rooster added to the symphony. The entire yard was growing restless. Just then, a few labourers appeared in the compound. One of them forged a smile, clearly disappointed at finding Angad there. "Is the landlord not here?" one asked. "I haven't seen anyone here. I came here an hour ago. Your landlord is still not taking my calls," Angad continued, "I wanted to give him a big surprise." A middle-aged woman reluctantly closed in on Angad. Holding a basket over her hip she kept hurling questions at him, "Hey young man, what is your name?" She showed her teeth, stained with tobacco. The woman was curious to know more about Angad. What did he do? What was his job? What was his salary? Was he married? Angad enjoyed the way she kept him engaged. In between, she kept praising his employer. "Prasad *anna* is the most progressive farmer in the entire area," she said while placing a *paan* leaf coated with lime and stuffed with fresh tobacco into her mouth and then wiping her hands clean on her saree. The lady did air her concerns in between, "It is unusual, for them not to be up and about by this time. Where have they all gone? They don't sleep so late!"

A male worker shouted, "Rohini *akka*, are you heading to the farms with these implements? Or are you wasting time with someone who has come to trouble our master?" Rohini retaliated, "You get lost! I know how to serve my master. I have been working for him since you were here around in a loincloth with a runny nose." Her remarks silenced the man. Rohini had a point to make. "You know the elder daughter of Prasad *anna* and you will make a good pair;" she whispered mischievously and quickly left.

Angad managed to hide his blush rendered by this sudden change in subject. Most recovery officers did their work exactly as per bank protocol. Yet, Angad always got emotionally close to his clients.

He waited for another ten to fifteen minutes or so, restlessly sitting in the old chair. Just then, one of the labourers came screaming, running from the backyard. She cried as if she was possessed and fell on the floor. There was chaos. By the time Angad could gather himself, dozens of people gathered, screaming, calling out someone or the other, breaking the house doors and windows with crowbars and hammers. Angad was shell-shocked at the sudden turn of events. Prasad, his wife and two children were lying in the dining area. Some yellow foam was oozing out of their mouths. The insecticide could be smelt from a distance. A farmer and his beloved family that fed urbanites for a meagre return, lay there dead. Angad lost control. His knees trembled; his vision blurred out. People from the entire village and even the neighbouring villages gathered around. Ambulances, police jeeps, and politicians representing different parties thronged to the house. Angad wept. Rohini appeared by his side and whispered: "Don't stay here! Just disappear!" Angad had no memory of leaving the house.

People started talking about the cause of the suicide. They spoke of harassment by the bankers to repay the debt, which drove Prasad to take the extreme step. They also mentioned a young man often visiting for recovery.

The identical faces of the two girls in their teens were visible behind the cobweb. They would have returned from school, changed their uniforms, and jumped among the heaps of hays with their friends in the yard, without ever knowing what was in store for them that night. What had transpired that fateful night? Maybe Prasad planted the idea. A shortcut to save himself from the debt and protect his honour.

The previous evening, Prasad's wife had attended the phone call that Angad made to hint towards a solution in his visit the next day. That was the time she understood the seriousness of the bank issue. However, on hearing Angad, she was overjoyed; expressed her gratitude; and promised to meet the next morning. She had colluded with Angad to give her husband a big surprise. But little did she know that Prasad would give her a bigger surprise, rather a shock which would leave the village, the bank, and everyone lost for words. Did Prasad's bullocks, cows and calves know anything of their loss? Would they mourn the absence of their master? Would they feel his absence? Prasad was the last farmer Angad dealt with, being a bank officer. He knew that he too had unknowingly abetted the unfortunate step taken by Prasad.

The scent of flowers filled the room. He could hear the tinkling of the silver anklets of Prasad's daughters. The sound of their giggles echoed in the room long after they were gone.

CHAPTER FOUR

Narendra Prasad was called by several names. His mother called him 'Naren' with a musical tone. His friends called him 'Nari,' which he liked. His father generally called him Naren. If he called him Narendra Prasad -- his full name with a high pitch, it was always in anger.

Narendra was poor in his studies. His dream was to land a secured army job like his father. He attended every recruitment drive in and around his place. However, despite his strong physical stature; he could not make it. Despite all odds, he managed to complete his matriculation. Some moderation marks owing to his father being an army man had come to his rescue.

A few years went by in his life, doing menial jobs. He did not take up a single job seriously and kept switching. Stints like a year at a cloth merchant in the town, a few years with a hardware shop and some with a courier company didn't give him any stable income.

During one of his annual vacations, his father recommended he marry his friend's daughter so that he could settle and take care of their land. Both friends had decided to marry their children with each other. It was only a ritual that Narendra Prasad was asked to visit the girl's house so that he could see her. He was asked to take one of his friends along. Thus, they both went to the address provided by his father. His mother wasn't fully convinced by the idea of Narendra's father in their son's marriage at such an early age. But she too thought that marriage might help her son settle down for good.

Several fritters and bakeries were laid on the wooden table. Too many plates of snacks for two men in their early twenties. This was something new for both the young lads. They had never experienced such respect and attention before.

An even younger lean girl was standing at a distance. Being extremely shy and not knowing what exactly to do, Narendra Prasad could not look at her. A ruffian cat moved around. It scratched Narendra Prasad's knee often and meowed repeatedly. Fritters fell down, tea spilt, and the girl giggled and ran inside. Both the young men got embarrassed and left the house.

He couldn't even ask the girl's name. It was only later that he got to know the girl's name who was going to be his partner for a lifetime; when he heard his parents talking about the girl. Sarayu, the name flowed like a river over his lips. He loved to say that again and again. The more he repeated that name; the more tender feelings arose in him.

The friends had already decided. It was just a formality. No one even asked for Narendra Prasad's opinion. And neither did he have one. All the elders got busy. They planned everything. The wedding was scheduled in six months, as his father had to resume his duty in the army. The girl and the boy were not allowed to meet until the marriage. And neither of them wanted to meet the other. They had not even seen each other properly. They had not talked to each other. The troublesome cat had not given any chance to Narendra to look at Sarayu properly. Probably, the decision was made in heaven.

After nearly six months, the entire village celebrated the wedding amidst long rituals. People witnessing the wedding made fun of the tender boy and girl who barely had crossed their legal marriage ages. They wondered how the young pair would start a family life together.

After a few days of marriage, the husband shifted to the wife's house, as per the understanding. He had a new duty of taking care of the family's land. He was pushed into it but with his silent consent. He stood at the end of the vast farmland and wondered what lay ahead.

Narendra Prasad was honest. And that made him the blue-eyed boy with his in-laws. The father, mother, daughter and son-in-law lived like a close-knit family. There was no discrimination. Narendra Prasad was not treated like an outsider even though he was from a different family. He soon became so attached to the new environment that he seldom remembered his family.

Sarayu was advised by her intelligent mother to delay conceiving a child by one or two years. Her mother did not want the young lady to take the burden of becoming a mother so quickly. This had worried Narendra Prasad until he knew it was a deliberate delay and not any biological concern.

Time is felt differently by different people. Here, the time went by quickly. The cycle of seasons came and went by. Sarayu's father went in flames within one season. It was expected. He had developed some chronic illness that kept him feeling down. As Narendra started taking care of responsibilities one after the other, his father-in-law was preparing himself for his retirement. The more confident he became; the more prepared he grew subconsciously to leave the world forever. His thought that he was no more needed, invited illness and he surrendered to it. He often expressed satisfaction over his honest son-in-law taking care of the household.

When seasons come and go, everything around gets seasoned and tuned.

The transformation was gradual and natural, from the boyish groom and a shy husband who couldn't even present himself to his new partner, to a seasoned man taking care of his mother-in-law and wife.

To fill the vacuum created by Sarayu's father, her mother wanted Sarayu to conceive at the earliest. Her mother wanted a grandchild. She found a reason to survive, a reason to hang on to this world. Without a desire, there is no tomorrow.

When all the lights in the house were turned off in the night, Sarayu held Narendra close and shyly, yet proudly with a sense of satisfaction, declared that she had conceived. Narendra felt a sense of fulfilment. He cried in happiness, held her close and kissed her all over. However, somehow Narendra did not feel comfortable with what he was doing. The expenditure for the farm was mounting. He wondered how his father-in-law made any profit after harvesting. He could not hide his discomfort, and it was visible to Sarayu. One night, after retiring to bed, he moved the feathery cotton saree from Sarayu's belly swollen with another budding life and kissed it repeatedly. The lights were off. Sarayu ploughed her fingers over his hair. "Is something wrong?" she asked softly. He responded in a negative tone. But then, quickly added, "Looks like, but…" "You are too tired after long walks on the farm. Now, hold your baby and sleep," she whispered into his ear. He pressed his head over her big belly and held her palm, weaving the fingers together.

The previous harvest was bountiful according to some of the labourers. Yet, the sale proceeds were not enough to clear the dues of the labourers, fertiliser shops, seed shops, etc. Somewhere, something went wrong. More money was required to bridge the gap.

For the farming activities, the labourers seemed to know almost everything. However, Narendra had no one to talk to on the money front.

And his father-in-law had single-handedly managed it, and none in the family knew how he did it. Narendra was perturbed. But he tried to pose a pleasant figure before his expecting wife and mother-in-law. Narendra decided to surrender to Gopal on the issue. Gopal is a senior labourer and seems to have many years of experience. So, one day he set out to Gopal's house in the evening. His house was small yet neat and clean. Narendra's visit delighted Gopal. An excited Gopal struggled to clear the veranda for his master to sit.

Narendra had no one to talk to, about the unmatching equations he was facing as he had no close friends. His life essentially was around his farm and family.

Gopal's wife, a dark-complexioned slender woman in her fifties or so, came and stood at a distance. She looked anxious upon the visit of Narendra, as it was for the first time that the landlord had visited their house. Both Gopal and his wife were expecting some news from Narendra. Narendra managed to diffuse the anxiety and asked Gopal to join him for a short walk. It was unusual. However, Gopal followed his master, maintaining a safe distance, often reminding him to know the purpose of the master's visit.

Walking by the narrow, uneven road in the village, Narendra began "Gopal, you know the harvest was good, but the money I received is not enough to pay the wages and other dues. I don't know what to do?" "What shall I say, *Anna*?" Gopal was puzzled as the landlord consulted him to resolve this issue. "You are a big man. You must be having a solution, *Anna*!" he said, showing a confused face. "Gopal, you might know how uncle managed in such times." There was a short span of reflective silence. Suddenly Gopal burst, saying-- "*Anna*, pledge some gold and take a temporary loan. We can repay the loan and take the gold back after the next harvest." Narendra liked the way Gopal said, "We can repay." It made him feel that there was someone with him in distress. However, he wasn't sure about taking that step to fill the financial gap.

After a hard day's work, the labourers returned to their houses, tired and sick. Some of them were seemingly tipsy. Narendra and Gopal consumed some locally made arrack that was made available by Gopal.

On his way back, Narendra started conspiring to borrow money from a pawnbroker recommended by Gopal. He had a finger ring and a chain that Sarayu gave him during their wedding. Sarayu would not allow pledging these things which are precious to her. And that too at a time when she is expecting. She might even consider it as a bad omen. That night after all the lights were turned off, Sarayu caught her man with the stink of the arrack distilled in the village. She loved the smell of the illegal distillate. She found something manly in the scent and tried to get more of it from his lips and his thick moustache. Narendra tried his best to get closer to his offspring without hurting it in the swollen womb. He forgot all his worries and drew himself to his offspring as closely as possible. There was only a thin wall of skin left between the father and the child. As he went closer to the belly and pressed his lips softly, Sarayu enjoyed the peak of satisfaction in the fulfilment of being a woman who could create a life within a life.

The next day Gopal came and started working without any indication of the previous day's meeting with Narendra. However, Narendra caught him and handed over his wedding ring and the chain.

Narendra went to Gopal's house in the evening to collect the money that he received for pledging the gold ornaments at the pawnbroker. The amount was not as expected. It was just enough to manage the labourers' dues and the tractor overhauling. The hospital expenditure anticipated against his child's delivery was still in question. However, he found some temporary solace.

Days passed. Sarayu gave birth to a beautiful, cherubic girl with eyes half-open. Narendra was euphoric, and he caressed its butter-like body all the time, sometimes even skipping his routine farm visits. Their family and the team of labourers rejoiced at the young one's arrival. Ceremonies continued to mark the blessing.

Narendra did not have any harvest for a few months, and therefore no income. The gold pledged was sold to get some more money. Sarayu could sense the difficulty but did not know its depth. Narendra robbed some ornaments from her too and pledged them. He promised her to take back the pledged gold soon. However, he doubted his promise.

Narendra put in his best efforts in the field and hoped to have a bountiful harvest this time too so that he could clear the dues. He spent a lot on several inputs, in an attempt to increase the volume of output. He consulted Gopal on almost everything in the absence of his father-in-law. Gopal consented to every action of Narendra. He had confidence in Narendra's honesty.

Some evenings, when the sky started darkening in the distance, Narendra walked towards Gopal's house for a round of the local fresh and steaming distillate. The strong and pungent smell of the arrack intoxicated Sarayu, and it pulled her to the other side of the young sleeping baby to get more of it. And she licked his firm lips and tasted it.

The pledged gold of Sarayu could not be taken back. Gopal had helped Narendra get a hand loan from the pesticide dealer to clear the pawnbroker's interest, renew the loan, and meet the ceremony expenditure. Debt was mounting, though gradually. The family gatherings and celebrations continued for a few more rounds.

A few months passed in a chain of hope and desperation. Narendra already had dues to the pawnbroker, pesticide shop and a couple of lenders introduced by Gopal. He tried his best to keep Sarayu unaware of the dwindling finance and let her enjoy pampering her child.

Now, Gopal brought up an idea to take a higher amount of loan from a bank under an agriculture loan scheme and pay all the smaller loans. They were making a large hole to close many small gaps. Narendra struggled with payment dues, fresh seed requirements, occasional tractor overhauling, fuel etc. Narendra was becoming a seasoned borrower. Sometimes, the harvest helped him bring down the debt level. With the high interest for the hand loans, it looked like there was no immediate end to his worries.

CHAPTER FIVE

Angad had begun to get used to his new life on the Hospital Street. Unlike his sleepy native town, the air did not stand still here. Everybody constantly seemed to be on the move. Life drove them. Or perhaps the need to survive pushed them.

Angad loved to stand on the balcony and observe. The monkeys were friendlier than he had initially thought. A few were regular visitors and would plant themselves on the parapet. He fed them peanuts and *chana*. Sometimes, he shared his breakfast with them. The monkeys competed amongst themselves when a few nuts were left on the parapet. It was a constant fight for survival, where the laws of the nature controlled animal world.

It had taken Angad over a year to heal the wounds of Prasad's disturbing suicide and his family's marginal escape from the jaws of death. Initially, Angad was so shocked that he wasn't able to process the situation. He believed that all four in Narendra's family were dead. It brought him solace when after a few weeks later, he found out that Prasad's wife and his daughters had miraculously survived the suicide bid. Perhaps, nothing happens without any reason; everything happens by some actions of ours, like in the case of Prasad

-- his spending pattern, inappropriate accounting practices and hiding the truth of his financial debts had led him to take such a drastic step.

The media made headlines with Narendra Prasad's suicide. Every time a news anchor presented a piece of news about a farmer's death or suicide elsewhere in the country, Angad was disturbed. He was convinced that it would continue to haunt him until his last breath.

Whenever Angad recollected the scene of the four members lying on the floor with their faces covered in yellow-coloured froth, he could still smell the deadly pesticide around him. They had easy access to the toxic chemicals that finally took away a farmer's life, leaving his family to suffer.

The monkeys jumped on the Gulmohar branches covered in colourful blossoms, beautiful sight to behold. Tactfully suspending himself on a low-hanging branch with one hand, the monkey scratched itself, looking at other monkeys above him. A few moments later, they all disappeared.

Angad glanced at a cute face in a bright red chequered uniform, holding a man's hand, waiting for the bus. The man must be her father. She often turned around and waved to her mother, who was standing on the neighbouring balcony of the same building. It presented a perfect picture of pure affection between a mother and child. The young girl's face resembled someone he had seen somewhere. The girl continued to wave, and her mother responded. The child boarded the bus guided by her father. While climbing the steps of the bus, she turned and waved one last time, expressing unhappiness on leaving for school. Holding the steel rails on the steps, she shook her head with ponytails, still looking at her mother. Her father handed over a bag full of books, a bottle of water and a snack box to his daughter before the bus left.

The bank management had supported Angad's decision to quit his job. They felt he was over-emotional and unfit for the job of recovering loans.

More than once, he had sought money from his mother, and she had obliged. It would be inappropriate to ask her repeatedly. Angad's mother wanted him to return and stay with them. She would try and convince him that his father too wanted him to return. There was always an antagonism between the father and the son. Nothing serious, but even a casual conversation between the two would end up in a heated argument.

The thought of another bank job was despicable to him. He also knew he would not be able to get any other kind of job. Even if he were offered a job, it would most likely be in the recovery department. He hated hearing stories of financial debts. He disliked listening to the personal problems of people. He wished that no family should suffer from any financial debt and that every family lives in abundance. A jobless, tired and sick Angad would spend all his time either in the room or on the balcony.

The main entrance to the casualty ward of the hospital was visible from the balcony. Most days the scenes in front of the casualty ward were grievous. Those visuals triggered penetrating thoughts in him. When Angad had had enough of watching people from the balcony, he would slip into a pair of jeans and saunter up and down the Hospital Street. He would soon return, realising that it was comfortable to watch from the balcony rather than walking on the uneven footpath encroached by hawkers selling fruits, snacks, footwear, imitation jewellery etc., and a host of permanently erected counters.

Within a short span of time, Angad made an instant connection with Noyola, the cute girl from the next door. Did Noyola resemble one of the daughters of Prasad, even though they were of different ages? Angad found scores of similarities between the two; the way she kept her hair neatly braided, the colourful hairpins she used; the way she chuckled.

Perhaps, people are the same. Often, he would feel that everyone has similar traits. The body language of both Noyola and Prasad's daughter seemed the same, their reactions to any situation were nearly the same. After several days of waving at her, Angad once met her while climbing the apartment steps. Angad smiled and greeted the young girl. However, the young girl was indifferent and moved on. The next day, Angad was hesitant to wave at Noyola when he spotted her at the bus stop with her father. Her mother, as usual, was standing on the balcony and waving at her. All these days, when Angad waved his hand, the girl never seemed to notice him. She only gestured towards her mother.

Days passed. The monkeys visited regularly barring a couple of days in between, for reasons unknown. Hundreds of people walked by the Hospital Street. They belonged to different geographical regions. They all kept talking or listening on their cell phones while on the move. They wore sarees, frocks, jeans, and dhotis, in all kinds of hues and colours. Hundreds of merchandise were sold daily by the hawkers on the footpath, sustaining their livelihoods. Deafening cries of relatives and friends of those who lost their battle to life were heard many a night.

It became an irresistible routine to wave at Noyola every morning. Angad waited every day, at the exact time, to bid goodbye to the little girl. Some days, Angad's expression became so loud that Noyola's mother noticed him on the balcony. Noyola's mother loved the care expressed by Angad for her daughter. A door opened for conversation.

Pleasantries were exchanged. Noyola's father-- Peter, appeared unfriendly. He hardly talked to anyone in the entire building. Peter drank heavily every evening. Once Angad met him in an inebriated state on the steps. He was finding it difficult to climb the steps. Angad greeted him and attempted to hold him from falling. Peter did not like it. He stared at Angad unpleasantly. Since then, Angad did not attempt to talk to Peter. Peter always maintained a distance from others. He appeared self-centred. If Peter was ever seen with a pleasant face, it was when his daughter was around. Even though Angad himself had numerous personal issues and unfinished tasks, he was curious about Peter's family. He checked with Raghu, who made unannounced lightning visits once or twice a week. Raghu had no idea of any of the occupants in the apartment. He himself was a guest in the apartment.

The little girl refused to show any friendliness except when with her parents. Angad's efforts to befriend the little girl went in vain. Whenever she came across the steps along with her parents, Angad greeted her but she never responded. Days after days counting it to weeks and months passed by. Noyola's mother flashed a smile or two whenever their eyes met in the morning during the daily waving session. Angad felt a great victory being able to break the ice with Noyola's family.

"My deep desire to develop a friendship with Noyola's family has met the laws of attraction," he thought to himself, getting some strange pleasure from believing that he deliberately attracted what he wanted.

It was a hot Sunday in the summer. Raghu was not in town. The monkeys hadn't visited yet. The Gulmohar looked dull. There were very few people moving around in the Hospital Street. Hotel Anand Bhavan on the other side had a good rush. The piping hot lentil *sambar* aroused Angad's palate as he inhaled deeply. A lone monkey sat on the parapet, relaxed and calm. Angad got some grains from the kitchen and put them before the monkey on the parapet.

As usual, Angad pulled the chair to the corner and kept himself busy watching the street. He could still recollect the taste of the *idli* and *sambar* he had from Anand Bhavan that morning. He hadn't decided what to do next. Getting another job was the last thing on his mind. He kept looking for an NGO with no work pressure, unlike what he had in his previous job. Angad had hardly come across anyone who ever spoke of having enough wealth. With no means of income, Angad's bank balance plunged. Urgent replenishment was needed. If nothing worked out, he would have to ask Raghu for a favour or approach his mother again which would then lead his father to intervene and give a sermon on having quit his otherwise enviable job, for no mistake of his. Angad was not critical of his father's occasional advice. He believed that his father had every right to advise him but it wasn't easy to accept his lectures at the critical phase he was in.

A large goods vehicle arrived and halted under the Gulmohar tree, shaking a few small branches and dropping lots of bright cherry-coloured flowers. A few uniformed men jumped out of the truck and headed into the apartment. Some families must be shifting out. Angad did not personally know any of them so it didn't matter to him who vacated.

Nearly two hours later, the truck was filled with furniture and a host of household things. The workers covered the truck with a thick tarpaulin sheet. The engine started with a lot of noise. The uniformed labourers managed to get onto the truck and adjust themselves among the spaces left between the haphazardly and precariously placed goods.

The monkeys had left. Butterflies and bees too left the trees, maybe due to the increasing heat. A colony of worker ants was still moving around, marching to show their strength and unparalleled discipline.

Soon a young couple got into the front seat of the truck. Angad recognised them. They were staying on the ground floor. Angad had once interacted with the man. Mr. Haldar was from Kolkata and worked for some defence establishment. Angad figured out that they were vacating the house and shifting elsewhere. No one was there to see them off. The truck moved along the Hospital Street. Angad watched the vehicle until it disappeared.

Mr. Haldar had no friends. He always moved around, lost in his thoughts and pensive. Behind his black thick oval eyeglasses' frames was an unpleasant face. His neatly combed hair and his long kurta made him look like a sober person. He never smiled at anyone, and therefore, no one smiled at him.

Whatever you give the same comes back to you, and it seems like a basic theory of the universe. For a moment, Angad maintained a neutral stand. He assured himself: "I should be behaving with people the way I wish them to be with me."

The world seems to run on some specific rules. And if we know the rules, life could be smooth. You attract what you desire deeply. What you get is what you give out. Our thoughts create the world. The thoughts of every little thing in the world today come together to create tomorrow. It sounded amazing. "Am I a creator too?" Yes, it is certain! Our thoughts constantly create the world. Angad tried to hold his thoughts for a moment, something against the natural process. He thought to himself, "I am a part of this thinking world; it is impossible to go against its rules. I cannot have a mind without thoughts. However, I can surely have a mind focused on something."

The bell in the neighbouring temple rang, followed by a conch being blown that reverberated all around. The sacred sound of Om echoed. Angad felt a stream of current passing down his spine. Standing on the balcony, he felt as if he was melting into the world. He looked down the street to see his reflection in the people walking there. He saw himself in them; he saw himself in the crows perched on a branch of the Gulmohar.

Numerous things are happening around us. Every incident calls for a natural reaction. "How can I save myself from this chain of thoughts," he thought to himself. "Maybe, that is the reason why wise old men lived like recluses in the forests and mountains. They kept themselves away from the daily botherations, resorting to a calm and tranquil existence. The mind can be still, only if the world around is still." The world around Angad turned tranquil. He felt drowsy and hit his bed.

CHAPTER SIX

The cows and buffalos stood still. Tears constantly ran down their faces. They did not make any noise when their fodder was delayed. They looked at each other, felt the emptiness and mourned. They had lost their caring master who cared to give quality fodder in time. He touched and caressed them as he moved around them. His sudden absence made them disinterested in food and water. They took many days to come to terms.

The entire region was engulfed with sorrow. The usual crows and mynas disappeared. Even the sun didn't appear as if it was mourning the unfortunate incident. Dark clouds pregnant with tears of sorrow surrounded the area. The gloominess stayed for several weeks.

The three who miraculously survived could not come to terms with the loss of Narendra. They sobbed in the dark corners, often mourning their departed one. They were all dependent on him. They loved the comfort and shade provided by the large tree. They had never imagined that their veranda, front yard, corridors, and rooms would one day be without him. They still wished that Narendra appeared out of the wall or the pillars. The emotional trauma created a deadly silence all over. A few labourers visited daily, did some chores around the house, and left without talking to anyone in the house. Their eyes remained welled up all the time. Some of them went to the field to take care of the standing crops. They did their tasks without waiting for instructions and without expecting anything. Such was the deep bonding they had with their former master. One of the labourers was heard saying that she would have offered her land and building had she known that the master was in such a financial crisis.

A few weeks later, some minor harvesting took place. Gopal waited for a nod from his master's wife to sell the produce at the market in the absence of his master. He was instructed to follow the usual practice. Gopal sold the grains, placed the bunch of rupee notes on the old carved wooden teapoy and stood vulnerable expressing his honesty.

Even though still stuck in a deep well of sorrow, she felt that the price she received was too less for the quantity mentioned. However, she did not comment. She believed that her loyal labourers would never under-report the income. Her children were mute spectators. For a moment, she thought that if she had a male child, it would have been easier for her to handle issues like these.

Gopal maintained attendance of labourers on a small piece of paper with their names and numbers written and scratched several times. Some workers did not regularly attend when they found that there was no direction from anyone. They just loitered around the house and returned. There were uncertainties. But they did not look worried. Gopal took some lead and planned to plough the land as an important requirement. He wished that his master's wife would give some instruction. Even none of her relatives showed up after a few months.

One day early in the morning, Gopal called on Sarayu and declared -- "*Akka*, there is a good amount of water in the canal, and I have ploughed all the wetland. We need seeds, and we must clear the seed seller's old dues to get new seeds." "Gopal, take this money and manage it," Sarayu handed him the cash Gopal had given her a few days ago. "If you want more, I have my ornaments," her voice broke. Hiding the tears in her eyes, she went inside the house. Gopal was elated at the trust shown by his mistress. "*Akka*, call your elder daughter. I don't know bookkeeping and how the master had done it. She is a brilliant student, and I need help in accounting." He managed to act brave, but his voice could not.

As soon as Sarayu called, both the girls came running. The mother and her caring daughters, Nanditha and Namitha, developed an even closer bonding after the departure of Narendra. Their collective experience of facing death together made their bonding even more robust. They were inseparable from each other. They ate together, slept on the same bed and stayed together. Nanditha was blank but curious to take over a new responsibility. Namitha put her hands around her elder sister to express her support. They were forcing themselves into it, even though the girls had no idea about it. But they were ready to roll around in the soil.

CHAPTER SEVEN

The scorching summer began, and the mornings lost their sheen without the children dressed in colourful attire, waiting for their school buses. The bright red flowers of Gulmohar covered the Hospital Street. The carpet thickened when the monkeys jumped from branch to branch. The flower showers provided a healing effect to the confined patients who looked through the windows of the Mission Hospital.

Crushing the soft petals under its dirty wheels, a mini goods vehicle came to a halt below the Gulmohar. It was loaded with an old wooden cot, a chair with white plastic netted seating, a gas stove, a cooking cylinder and many small packages which looked like kitchen utensils—a few large-sized wooden frames with canvas along with rolls of paper were also stacked among the goods.

Maybe a new family was coming to occupy the vacated house. After all, Hospital Street was such a happening place; any property would not remain vacant for more than a week.

The vehicle was parked there for close to two hours. The van driver and his aide had disappeared. Angad was hesitant to leave the balcony. He wanted to see the new residents, hoping they were friendly unlike most of the existing inmates in the building.

Most people who lived in Sabari Apartment did not care for each other. Only a few greeted each other when they met in the corridor or walked up and down the staircase. Angad spent a lot of time on the balcony. If he did go inside the house looking for something, he rushed back outside to continue his vigilance. Soon a couple followed in an autorickshaw. The slender woman moved to a secluded spot on the footpath. A man in a below-knee-length, long black kurta kept talking on his cell phone even while he paid the auto driver. He sported a long unkempt salt and pepper beard. Slim and tall, he looked perfect in the long kurta. His drawn-in cheeks and long grown messy hair gave him a nerdy look.

Some men emerged from the crowd and started shifting the luggage into Sabari Apartment. From the balcony, Angad could view the upper portion of the goods being moved in.

Soon the lady went missing. The man lit a cigarette and blew the smoke out without even caring for the people around him. The men engaged in shifting were in a hurry. They started shouting at each other to speed up, sometimes hurling abuses for not keeping pace. They maintained a rhythm, and in a short time, they had shifted everything into the building. When the labourers moved some trunks, the man helped them and warned them to handle the trunks carefully. It looked like they were precious to him.

The man put out his cigarette and engaged in some negotiation with those people before paying them off. Minutes later, the man too melted into the apartment. He might join his partner in arranging the house. The repeated movement of the vehicle and the labourers crushed the fresh flowers of the Gulmohar tree into a mushy paste.

Raghu returned home in the evening after many days. He was on an auditing tour to Mangalore. He would be home with Angad for three to four days before going off for his countryside auditing. He looked tired with worn-out eyes.

Angad was happy to have Raghu back. He finally had someone to talk to and spend time with. Raghu would narrate stories about his travels. He would face many problems in a small town, non-availability of good food, and how the local government officials tried to save themselves from discrepancies he had uncovered. The days Raghu was home, they talked for hours.

A phone conversation with his mother took Angad back to the family he had been missing for a long time. Yes, it had been a long time since Angad had moved to the city. Nothing had changed since then. Since the time he came to the Hospital Street, he never went back home. Whenever his mother insisted, he made some excuses.

At home, his mother was always in and around the kitchen. She was either cooking or preparing for the next meal. After every meal, there was elaborate planning for the next meal and it continued endlessly. Meenakshi, his mother had a unique cooking skill; a natural talent to cook and make any dish delicious with the touch of her magical hands.

Angad's parents lived for each other. His mother had placed his father close to her heart. It was a submission unto him. To step out of the house, she took permission from him. She got up early in the morning to cook the food of his choice. By the time he got up, a steaming cup of black coffee with a portion of butter dropped on the surface would be ready. She would watch him enjoying the steaming beverage. Simultaneously, she would also keep a tab on the whistling cooker and then would gracefully send him for his routine morning walk by pulling his sandals from the rack, dusting them, and placing them in the foyer. Even if he went out for half an hour, she would see him off from the hall as if he was going out for a long trip.

After sending off her husband, she would be again back in the kitchen. With a juggler's skill, she managed to boil milk, steam *idlis*, and stir the boiling lentil curry while doing other jobs. She did not just cook for him, but instead, put her best efforts to make the most delicious food for him. She did not take it as a burden. Instead, she considered cooking for him as a part of her prayers.

Angad was unsure if they loved each other.

It seemed more like a duty towards one another. While one's task was to earn bread, the other's was a commitment to bake the bread.

Viswanathan, Angad's father was the only man in Meenakshi's life. The only man she knew. The ripples created by other boys in her life subsided after her marriage when she had barely crossed twenty. After marriage, when she came to Viswanathan's house, she was afraid of everything. She had sacrificed the giggling company of her close friends. She carefully moved around. She made attempts to please the in-laws. After moving in with her husband to a new house near the bank where Viswanathan worked, she confined herself to his service.

She loved his hairy chest, the smell of his sweat, his thick moustache, and his short coarse hair. She admired every inch of him. She enjoyed her life within the confines of the house. She knew peace was all that she wanted, and peace after having a caring husband and an offspring. She was always cautious about her *karmas*. She loved to be neutral in her thoughts. She believed only in one emotion, and that was love. Angad had never heard her make adverse comments about anyone or anything.

She made no opinion about anything. According to her, everything returns like a pendulum, and every cause-karma would bring an effect-karma. Vishwanathan laughed at his wife's philosophy.

"Every cause-karma brings an effect-karma, and this is what is constantly happening. But most of us don't realise and acknowledge it. Yet, that is the truth;" she spoke with conviction. Vishwanathan laughed again. Somewhere deep down in his mind, he felt what she said was true. However, his conscious mind did not allow him to accept it.

"Where did you learn it from?" Vishwanathan was surprised at his wife's wisdom about *karma*. In every action of hers, she practised the cause-and-effect factor. It was amazing to know that before she took any action or thought anything, she paused for a second and weighed the possible effect. Vishwanathan was still hesitant to accept his wife's blind logic but he was neither ready to dismiss the theory outright.

He too started observing how his behaviour or thoughts created everything that he experienced. Without telling his wife, he started practising conscious living. "I today decide what I should experience tomorrow, and accordingly, I will invest my causes," the banker told himself.

Weeks and months went by. It was only after experiencing the effects that he thought guilty of, having made a wrong cause. Peace is the ultimate for anything. Is that why Meenakshi often chants peace? A peaceful mind can consciously send out good causes, while an agitated mind carelessly sends out random thoughts without realising their possible effects. There are only causes and effects. People's perception makes it good or bad. Vishwanathan concluded -- even emotions are a biochemical process!

A year and a few months later, they had another reason to love. Meenakshi spent her whole day caring for her newborn, even enjoying the act of cleaning her little one's bottom. She enjoyed the feeling of the mother in her. For she knew, it was for this that she was living.

Her cradle songs to get the child to sleep always referred to the young naughty Lord Krishna. She pulled his cheeks and snuggled him to her chest. She prayed that the young boy accomplished every good thing in life and grow up as a kind-hearted man.

The day the young boy turned on his own and rested on his stomach, Meenakshi jumped with joy. She cried and called Vishwanathan. She was in tears. Out of satisfaction of fulfilment that evening, she buried her head into Vishwanathan's hairy chest and put her hands around his waist without hiding her tears.

The day she sent her son to kindergarten, Meenakshi stood at the gate until the school got over. Like any mother, she too was concerned about Angad's comforts at home and in school. In the noon, when the boy returned, she hugged him tightly. Thus, she enjoyed every moment of her fulfilling life.

Every time Angad was bathed in water warmed with herbs, she put a black kohl dot on his right cheek to ward off the evil eyes. If a guest commented on the boy's cuteness, immediately after the guest had left, Meenakshi would take a dried chilli and a pinch of mustard in her palm, encircle it around his face chanting to ward off the after-effects of the evil eye. She did all this to safeguard her child from the evil gaze of the guests.

Meenakshi's fulfilling life orbited around Vishwanathan and Angad. One who supported her in every moment despite being short-tempered. And the other one being raised by her, meticulously, to be a well-admired gentleman. Watching him grow was fun for her. Within no time, he grew from wearing knickers to long pants. And then, within the blink of an eye, he turned into a man.

Angad was always his mom's son. The bonding between the mom and son developed naturally. There was an invisible gap between Angad and his father. For reasons unknown to both, their ideas never matched. Every time his father would approach him, he announced his arrival with a fake cough. Upon hearing it, Angad would go to his room or to the dining room to escape getting caught. If spotted, his father would throw a volley of questions about Angad's studies, his money-spending pattern and everything that came to his mind at that point in time. If proper and instant answers were not provided, his father would get annoyed. His father would turn to his mother, and finally, a cold war would pursue. During such times, she gave a break to her *karma* theories!

His fake cough was a blessing indeed. It helped Angad escape his father's rage most of the time. Angad was a rebel against his father for no reason. He never hated his father. He had all the love for him. However, his father's anxiety always irritated him. Angad's father never supported his banking career with a rural posting. He wanted Angad to work in big cities, which would help him get better exposure. The tragic incident in Angad's career made his father comment that his disobedience caused a fracture in his career.

Life with his parents was somewhat different. Despite minor discords, both his parents cared for him. He stayed for close to two decades with them. This was the first time that he had moved away from them for this long.

This season, the spring lasted longer. Each flower that bloomed on the Gulmohar tree on the Hospital Street had a life similar to any other human being. Every flower had a short but complete life.

For Angad and Yamini, the spring continued. The laws of nature brought them together; the laws of attraction brought them together. Despite knowing the illegitimacy, they continued. Their world did not care about society and its rules.

Angad was intoxicated by the way Yamini Peter's eyes glowed every time she looked at him. The glow was extraordinary. The conversation on the edge of two balconies gradually shifted inside the house.

Yamini dressed up every morning to meet Angad on the balcony. She waited for her husband to leave home before she went to the balcony to meet Angad. She would choose her clothes carefully. Angad felt intoxicated by Yamini's radiance.

They spent hours together on the balcony watching the world move by. He felt guilty and confused. But when he met her, the pleasure subsided his guilt. The Gulmohar, monkeys, birds and ants were witnesses to the illicit association between Mrs. Yamini Peter and Angad. Angad was well aware that a relationship with someone else's wife, someone else's mother, was the last thing he should desire. Yet, he was under the influence of some invisible power.

Hospital Street was relatively peaceful on Sunday mornings. The number of vehicles plying was less which made those who walked, happy. They could enjoy the pleasant morning breeze along with the birds chirping.

A blue and white coloured ambulance vehicle sped past, sounding alarm bells with a revolving beacon. Most other vehicles gave way to the ambulance. The vehicle drove straight into the casualty section of the hospital. A few minutes later, a group of people gathered at the entrance of the casualty section. They cried inconsolably. Surely, there was some bad news.

CHAPTER EIGHT

The first harvest under Nanditha's control was a letdown. The expenditure and returns did not match, which sent her into deep contemplation. She talked to her mother Sarayu, and Sarayu had no idea how it could match. The income cannot be lesser than the expenditure. Gopal, as usual, showed his palm as if he was not a stakeholder in the business at all. To him, farming was a ritual. He came everyday morning, caressed the obedient bullocks on their back and forehead and gradually picked up doing one or the other thing before picking pace. He and his team did everything as a ritual. Perhaps they didn't consider this as work which could bring them wealth.

Nanditha was depressed to the core. She went on a meeting with many farmers in the village and around. Most of them depended on pure luck rather than a planned activity to generate wealth. Someone took the name of Mr.Siddique, the area agriculture officer from the government. Siddique's eyes were wide open when Nanditha reached him and sought some professional assistance for the next crop. Siddique stroked his bald head in contemplation and promised to help the girl.

Siddique was an honest officer. Though he doubted the young girl's enthusiasm and readiness to go ahead with caution, he was delighted to extend assistance. The following day, he reached Nanditha's house with a few tools. Accompanied by the girl, he went to the farm; took a few soil samples, and said he would first analyse the soil before giving any suggestions. The labourers were amazed to see something new happening.

Siddique was a book of farming knowledge and practices. If it was Angad in the past as a guest for breakfast, now it was Siddique. He savoured the steaming breakfast cooked by Sarayu before rushing to the field with her daughter. Awestruck labourers watched the duo checking things and jotting something in the notebook - something they had never experienced in the past. Siddique helped the girl at every step. She became his ardent fan and found a hero in him. The young, smart man soon became her ideal man, and she secretly nurtured a special space for him in her mind. The thought of him tickled the cupid in her.

A few months ahead, the family received a good harvest assisted by the agricultural officer. He also helped in finding new buyers. This time, after tallying the account, they could find some small profit. That minor improvement was significant in building confidence.

Sun shined brighter than usual. Nanditha was waiting for her ideal man and the delay in his arrival made her impatient. She loved every piece of advice given by Siddique. He had already taught her the principles of scientific and planned farming, and she got a clear idea about managing soil, seeds, and other farm inputs. In her heart, too, she secretly cultivated a desire. The pull towards her ideal man was forceful, and she couldn't control it. The more she tried to control it, the more and more thoughts about him appeared.

Siddique had mentioned to Nandita during a conversation that he was married and had a young child. But that was not a factor for the cupid to pull back. She was unsure why she liked him and what she wanted from him. Nevertheless, she loved his bald forehead, thick black moustache and his smile that shed beaming light when he spoke. Her admiration knew no bounds. Sarayu suspected that her daughter was seeing him.

Nanditha started managing the farms well after a few seasons. Her fleshy cheeks got tanned by the scorching sun. The women labourers praised her flawless beauty and cautioned her not to step in the sun and protect her skin until marriage. "I can't think of marriage until I clear my father's debts," she retorted to those who talked about her marriage. "Yes, yes, you are a smart girl, and we will wait. And you are also too young to marry now," an old lady commented and giggled, expressing her love for the child. They loved the girl and her family. They were happy to see them gradually returning to normalcy after a few crop seasons.

Nanditha did not spare her younger sibling, who knew better than her about using the internet. Long before the harvest, Namitha started looking for buyers for the produce, some of them were direct consumers. Siddique had helped initially in locating such bulk buyers in the city. Some startups were of real help. The price recovery improved, and things were improving season after season. It had been more than two weeks since Siddique visited Nanditha's house. She was feeling restless and was longing for his presence. And when he arrived on Sunday morning, she managed to hide her excitement before her mother and others. Her eyes widened, and she wanted to know his whereabouts, much to the embarrassment of Siddique. Sarayu did not like Nanditha's growing closeness to Siddique but was afraid to warn her.

Siddique could sense the excitement in Nanditha's eyes when he visited her after a long gap. Her gentle complaint in a soft tone about the long gap made him worry. He decided to manage the girl tactfully and chose to stay away. While leaving their farm that day, he spoke to Nanditha; "Don't forget, you have a daunting task, and that must be your priority." Sarayu overheard it, shedding a few drops of tears over her smooth and shiny cheeks. She was sure of what would have transpired between the two. The decisive conclusion by Siddique was a great relief for Sarayu. Nanditha was at a ripe age and was vulnerable to any emotional challenges. Sarayu watched the gentleman through the casement window, kick-starting his bike and disappearing through the boundary gate.

Nanditha stood on the veranda, hiding her face on the side of the brown, aged wooden pillar. She did not want her mother or sister or even the labourers to see her swollen face and welled-up eyes. She took a few moments to bring her capricious mind in control. Siddique's words echoed in her ears. She wiped her face with her palms, cleaned her palms on her skirt, raised her head firmly and moved towards the field. Sarayu too wiped her cheeks.

CHAPTER NINE

Raghu was in Mangalore. He occasionally called to check on things and was thrilled to hear that Angad had got a new job.

Angad did not know the exact nature of his job. The start-up chief being on a shoestring budget and a Hobson's choice job were made for each other. A few articles published in a national daily was the only point in Angad's resume that helped him get the appointment.

Angad had found a new life. One needs a reason to wake up in the morning and kickstart one's day. Angad was back to nursery class rhyming and finding their new meanings.

It had been a few months since Yamini and Angad started getting along. From then on, Angad was rarely alone on his balcony. Despite knowing that this relationship would lead nowhere, they both continued. They both celebrated and indulged in what most viewed as forbidden.

A monstrous yellow-coloured earth mover was parked on the vacant land across the street. The bushes and plants shivered in fear owing to their towering presence.

The family that had occupied a corner of the plot was shifted onto the pavement next to the tiny temple. They sold earthen pots of various shapes and sizes, piled up on the plot where they lived. The family was now busy stacking their pots next to the temple. The man and his wife returned to the plot, time and again, to hunt for their unsold pots which were hidden in the bushes. With her runny nose smearing her cheeks, their daughter struggled to help the couple carry those pots without breaking them.

Angad thought about what the potter's horoscope for the week would have predicted: a change of home, from a makeshift plastic sheeted tent to the footpath.

The couple had occupied that piece of land for over fifteen years. The man brought earthen pots of different shapes, sizes, and shades from his village in Tamil Nadu, and sold them here for a profit. His business flourished especially during festive seasons like Diwali and Dussera.

One evening, many weeks ago, Raghu had mentioned the couple. He told Angad how the man lived alone and sold earthen pots mainly during festive seasons, till he met his beautiful future wife when a group of labourers came to pave the Hospital Road with asphalt.

There was a heavy downpour in the evening. Angad loved rain. Rain always brought a renewed sense of life. All the trees lining the Hospital Street swayed in the shower. A few branches came crashing down, snapping power cables and enveloping the area in eerie darkness.

A lantern struggled to provide light under the synthetic sheet that covered the temporary shelter where the potter and his family settled — each drop of rain that fell on the tent felt like a boulder falling on it. The night lasted long.

The Hospital Street looked serene and well-laid out for the day. With a steaming black tea in his porcelain cup, Angad stepped out onto the balcony. The light fog lifted as milk and newspaper delivery boys made their daily rounds. A new set of red ants celebrated the day by striding across the branches that were washed afresh by the previous night's showers. The potter and his family were not seen on the footpath. Their hut and the merchandise had vanished altogether. They must have moved to escape the fury of the rain.

The blend of deep red and black had a mystical effect on Angad. He felt the magical effect when Yamini draped herself in that incredible combination of colours. She turned into a goddess of beauty. The heavy necklace glittered around her slender neck. The large earrings swayed in perfect unison. She emanated a sensual fragrance. Angad melted every time she was in front of him. Wafting in the air came her captivating aroma before she arrived. She melted with Angad to become one as they moved around the balcony. The presence of the ants, monkeys, crows and pigeons made their union mesmeric. Earth, air, water, fire and space worked together to complete their blend.

The attraction towards Yamini was very strong. With each step forward, something inside him asked him to stop. He heard it. He hesitated. But he was pulled into the whirlpool of desires. He was engulfed by the laws of attracting the opposite.

Angad felt he had a flair for writing attractive and catchy product promotion titles or copies. But what he had thought of as an easy job, was not easy at all. He pondered for days on end to bring out the writer in him. He struggled to write notes that would create an impact.

Dozens of draft copies written night after night went straight into the dustbin. Angad found a complete absence of creativity. Words did not flow. Rejection of every piece that he struggled to write, put his job at peril. Angad continued to string words together despite his mind entwined in the fusion of red and black.

Angad spent more time with Yamini than with a pen. The breeze around the Hospital Street tickled their nerves. Both of them, hand in hand, flowed out of the rough balcony and strolled with tender, warm feelings to the end of the street. They continued their romantic expedition, and the clumps of ringed bamboos in the city parks offered them enough opportunities to be even closer. They lost their initial hitch and danced on their feet in time with the wind.

One evening a fight erupted at Peter's house, which lasted for hours. Noyola cried profusely for hours. On hearing the ensuing clatter, Angad was about to knock on their door when he heard Peter taking his name repeatedly. Angad stopped. It was clear that Peter had known about their alliance.

Angad returned to his room. He was ashamed of spoiling an otherwise seemingly happy family. He had made a big mistake. "We are not doing what we want to do. We are doing what nature wants us to do. Isn't that so?" he wistfully thought.

A few days later, Angad saw a large truck of movers and packers parked below the Gulmohar tree. The Gulmohar rustled in the wind, it shed a few flowers and prepared to witness some action.

The rent at Sabari Apartment, a government housing scheme apartment, was reasonable. And so, rooms for rent did not remain vacant for long. Proximity to prime locations was also a reason for continuous occupancy. Soon a new couple or a family would come to occupy the space that Yamini and Peter had called home. Her body odour and the mesmerising black and deep red combination will give way to new ones.

Angad admired Peter. Peter could have barged into his room and questioned him about their illicit relationship. But Peter cared only for his canvas and colours. He created the world he wanted on the canvas and didn't depend on the real world to present him the same. However, his canvas had no space for Yamini. Yamini was suffocated. The bright colours with their toxic smell choked her. She wanted a life beyond the frame of the canvas. She wanted to breathe fresh.

The *sambar* at Ananda Bhavan spread its aroma of blended spices. For most, a smell is always associated with a memory - the boiling *sambar's* smell was associated with that of home. Everyone around loved it and inhaled every bit of it.

CHAPTER TEN

It was an overcast Sunday. The sun played hide and seek through the window. Hospital Street was gradually waking up to the sounds of cawing crows settling on the trees. Yamini had left, leaving a vacuum and an immense feeling of guilt. Many pending assignments proved the copywriter's job as a challenge. Mental turmoil disturbed Angad's creativity, and he did not complete a single project to the team's satisfaction that would approve of his work.

Angad placed a few glistening sugar crystals on the parapet wall for the passing ants. He allowed them to savour it and climb over his palm. A few of them freely moved around his hands, chest and earlobes. "The insects, too, could have a thinking mind like us humans. Maybe, a family too. Perhaps, they too, are ambitious and desirous. Maybe, we can connect with them, for they are a part of this connected universe," thought Angad.

A pigeon on the parapet moved its eyes and cooed a few times. Angad gazed at the number of people walking on the Hospital Street. The pigeon periodically cooed, reminding Angad of its presence. Its curious eyes expressed anxiety. A red ant with a large garter moved around its hill. Angad went into a trance, in sync with every living being around;

visible and invisible creatures.

The mobile phone kept ringing an irritating beep, and Angad could not ignore it anymore. On the other side, an unknown voice asked him to reach home urgently, and it was not good news. Then Angad heard his mother's voice on the phone. She was trying to say something, but her wails drowned out her words.

"Amma..." he tried to interrupt her as she cried her heart out.

Amma's cries were similar to those heard from the Mission Hospital many a night. Did she mention 'father'? Angad was not sure. Did that phone ring differently this time? The street suddenly turned dark. The trees stood still. A crow, a pigeon, a few mynas, a couple of monkeys and countless ants lined up. They stood unified in grief. Angad's body weakened, his jaws stiffened, and he turned pale.

It took a few hours to reach home. Many known and unknown people had crowded outside. They were whispering. Angad stepped out of the car. Someone took his duffle bag and put a sympathising hand on his shoulder. A few led him inside the house.

There, on the cold ground, lay his hero, his villain, and the person he had learnt to love and hate at the same time. There he lay, lifeless. Angad thought he had not seen his father's face so close for years. His shrivelled skin showed how old he was. Yet, the death was untimely. He had many unfinished dreams; he had not seen his son get married and he did not become a grandfather and play with his grandchildren.

Angad touched the lifeless cheeks. And then the eyelids. One last time, he wanted to gaze into his father's eyes directly as it had been a while since they looked into each other's eyes and communicated.

Trivial issues had created friction very often. It wasn't anything serious, but there was a lack of harmony between the father and the son. They both repelled each other when they came close.

Someone placed his hand over Angad's back, trying to prevent him from opening his father's eyelids. His mother continued to sob, taking Angad's name in between. A few elders guided Angad on the rites that were to take place before the cremation. They were in a hurry to get it over with, worried about a change in the weather.

Angad followed whatever he was asked to do. He never realised how his home would be without the person who diligently built it. He was aware that all that his father and mother owned would one day be his and then his heir apparent. "Ownership is an absurd idea. What does it mean? The very word ownership is meaningless. We don't own anything. We hold it for some time and then leave, but that very feeling makes people different." – Angad thought.

Mother's sister was the last one to leave three weeks later. Mother sobbed now and then, even after so many days had passed. Her world revolved around her husband. She could not deal with the world without him. Angad sat in the living room silently, close to his mother. Sometimes, he struck up a conversation because the silence was deafening. His mother got reserved and spoke very little.

She moved around the house silently, finishing her chores. However, she now had a lot of free time at hand as the one she had been catering to was no longer around.

The grief gradually subsided. Meenakshi started being dependent on Angad. She waited for him to know what he would have for dinner. Until recently, his mother prepared everything keeping her husband's choice in mind. She had existed for her husband. She enjoyed the cool shade and comfort of her husband's existence, which one day came crashing down.

Meenakshi started finding a similar shade and comfort in her growing son. To ask him what to cook for dinner. To organise what he needed. She stopped wearing coloured sarees. Draping those dull sarees, she looked much older than she was, without her usual large red *bindi* on her forehead.

One day, she pulled a large metal trunk, called Angad to the living room, asked him to sit beside her and said, "I want to discuss something with you. Please sit here and listen to me carefully." It was more of an appeal. She started treating Angad as someone who would take care of and protect her from then onwards. Angad sat close to her and prepared himself to listen to what she was going to say. He was all ears. He presumed it to be a list of responsibilities that he had to take on.

The olive-green-coloured, generations-old metal box looked strong. An heirloom handed down from generation to generation. Its paint peeled off here and there. It smelt antic with its rusted padlock. Angad was not sure what it contained until his mother opened it.

A bundle of land documents, wads of money and some other papers were stuffed in the box. She took them out one after the other. The wads of cash had a white powder-like fungus all over them. Angad's mother dusted them with a cloth wipe and handed them to Angad. Angad accepted them. The documents were of the land, houses and other properties owned by Vishwanathan and Meenakshi jointly and individually.

"Your father was a hard worker. He saved and bought all these properties for you," her eyes glittered as she spoke of her husband's achievements. "Now you must maintain all these.

He bought this house in my name. See this." She showed him some other documents. She took every paper and explained the owner's credentials. She did not leave any opportunity to describe the troubles her husband had faced in acquiring the property. She brought out a dozen bank deposit receipts before she started sobbing, covering her face with the *pallu* of her grey-coloured saree. Angad pacified her.

It took her a few minutes to come out of the emotional plunge. Then she playfully said, "Take care of these assets, marry a girl next year and settle down." She looked into Angad's eyes keenly to know his response. She was disappointed seeing his expressionless face. Angad got up and moved towards the veranda. The wooden chair that his father occupied each morning and evening remained empty, inviting a new occupant.

For a moment, Angad saw him sitting there deeply engrossed, reading the printed lines in the newspaper.

A soothing breeze brought in a pleasantly intoxicating tobacco smell reminding him of his father once in a while. Angad's deep thoughts created a metaphysical form of his father next to him. He thought that it is one's thoughts that alter the physical world.

He took deep breaths, calmed himself and then imagined his father sitting on the wooden easy chair. He visualised his father's mix of black and grey hair, his thick moustache, firm cheeks, and bright eyes planted on the lines in the financial newspaper of the day, his legs crossed one over the other, white cotton *dhoti* and mandarin collared cotton shirt. Often, he shook the newspaper to be able to read better. Vishwanathan's presence gave the surroundings a fresh look. Angad took a deep breath to feel more and more of what he imagined.

Amidst the odour of fresh crispy potato fritters diffusing the air, he heard his mother calling him for the evening tea. "My life hereafter may take a different turn," thought Angad. He longed to return to his newfound abode at the Hospital Street. The spirited street with a canopy of Gulmohar. He wanted to return to those mute creatures, watch the school girls and boys as they waited for their school buses; the street vendors; the loud cries of the relatives for their deceased ones from the Mission Hospital. Other than his challenging copywriter's job, he missed everything.

Angad was unsure about his next move. Munching on the steaming succulent fritters, Angad asked, "*Amma,* what next?" With a mouthful of the bite, she took her sweet time to chew and swallow the fritter while pondering over Angad's question. However, even after a few more rounds of devouring the snack, she did not respond.

Did she not hear what I asked her? thought

Angad. Angad called her to gain her attention-- "*Amma...*" She raised her hand, signalling him to wait. When she completed the last drop of tea in the cup, she paused and looked pointlessly at the wooden chair on the veranda. Was she trying to delay a response? She said, "I return the question to you with a motherly gesture. It would be best if you take the lead from now on. Your father's pension is enough for me to live." Again, she said this, looking at the easy wooden chair with a hanging cloth and long arms, which seemed to sway for a second. She looked contented and composed.

Her response did not provide any way forward for Angad, and his question was still left unanswered. *Amma's* reaction was apparent in her case, but not for Angad, and there was no hint for Angad as to what he should do next.

They both felt that a third person was sitting in that chair and participating in the conversation without uttering a word.

With a blank mind, Angad leaned over the backrest of the settee. Mother got up and collected the empty plates and cups. She ran her fingers over his head and said, "You are old enough to take your own decision. I will live with you till my death or till the time your wife allows me to;" she added with a mischievous smile.

But "*Amma*, I need to go back to complete the assignments. Can you accompany me to the city for some time?"

Her answer came instantly-- "No, no, I cannot leave this house. You know your father is still here. I see him everywhere. I see him sitting in that easy chair in the veranda, relaxing in the settee, watching television, and sometimes asking me for a cup of tea." She continued, "Yesterday, I heard him walking around, the same that I used to hear whenever he returned from the bank in the evening. Morning, he had coughed in the bathroom. I could hear it."

For his mother, her husband was still present in the house. She wanted to believe that. She created his presence and continued a life projected according to her convenience and wishes.

A few days down the line, the dense fog over his immediate future lifted. Mother was ecstatic. She hummed songs from her young days. She continued to project the presence of her husband around her. She was happy.

Every time mother spoke, she resonated with an apt philosophical quote straight out of the Bhagavad Gita. An all-new *Amma* was in the making. Angad had misjudged his mother. He had never realised that his mother possessed such an understanding to cope with new situations.

His mother had started living in a new home created by her thoughts. She created it, and she herself became a part of the creation. She was casual and relaxed.

How did she acquire this unique skill of creating something out of thin air and being a part of it? She was so involved in her make-believe world that she sometimes showed gestures of the father's presence and even communicated with him. She cooked for her husband. Prepared lemon tea for him and left it near the wooden chair. She dusted his sandals and left them on the steps.

In a way, Angad was more than happy that his mother had become self-reliant in her thoughts.

After nearly a month, Angad returned to the Hospital Street. Raghu was there to receive him. Angad quickly went to the balcony to meet the cohabitants. The place was littered with dried leaves, and flowers, and amongst them were hundreds of ants and insects. His presence put most of them in panic, and they started running helter-skelter. Angad withdrew as he did not want to trouble the friendly creatures.

Raghu sat in the wooden chair jotting digits in a diary. He seemed lost between the pen and the diary. "Not tallying?" inquired Angad, looking at his pondering face. Raghu smiled and said, "You are still a bachelor. You don't need to worry like a married man." "Tell me, what happened now?"— asked Angad.

"Nothing much," Raghu kept his book and

pen aside, pushed the chair closer to Angad and said, "Next month, I need to arrange for my son's preschool admission. I worry about his mounting fees." Angad smiled. Raghu resumed his calculation and showed his frustration, still counting over his fingers. "I will have a few lean months as well," announced Raghu.

Everyone works for survival. The moment a person realises the need for supplies to survive, he becomes a money-making machine. After the realisation, it's a constant struggle for survival until the last breath. Look around, most people are talking about nothing other than wealth. And no one seems to be satisfied with what they have. Almost all the time, it's a complaint of the lack of it.

Once in a while, Raghu too complained about the little dearness allowance paid for his tours and the long-pending salary revision for central government employees. Most government employees are dissatisfied despite being paid so well, Angad contemplated.

"Raghu must be projecting a wealthy lifestyle just like how my mother does," Angad felt. Wealthiness is a state of mind. His mother had recently mentioned that one could feel rich with so little. And yet, one could still feel poor with billions. Richness is a state of the mind.

Angad's mother called him almost every day and, on some days, more than once. Even with all her positivity, she was lonely. She insisted upon Angad's return. On his return, he promised to complete his pending assignments and return home for good.

A new tenant now occupied flat number 203. Every time Angad faced its stained and dirty wooden door, he could smell Yamini's presence. The warmth of her breath, her intoxicating smell and her long, lush hair that smelt of coconut oil.

Angad was turning into a bit of an introvert. He slept whenever he felt like it, and he ate when hungry. Angad practised his newfound 'freedom' from monotonous routines set by society. Another breezy day dawned. He had lost interest in counting days or keeping a tab on time.

After a long walk to the cultural association building, Angad had just returned to the flat. It was exhausting. Pausing for a second to catch his breath on a step closer to flat number 203, he noticed a woman standing at the door waiting to welcome somebody. A blanket of dark, long hair swayed behind her. The woman stood there like a goddess with a sharp oval face, large and extended eyebrows, sensitive eyes, broad lips, and a vast temple. The woman, seemingly in her late twenties, was draped in a mesmerising combination of a bright red and black saree.

She looked authoritative with the blouse covering her neck and the sharp portrait-like features. She smiled at Angad. He did not expect that. "Why should someone smile without a valid reason at someone on seeing them for the first time?" Angad was a bit puzzled. "Was she waiting here for me?" he fumbled and returned a smile.

"Hello," she said. "I am Anuradha, the new tenant here." As she turned to speak, a gust of wind made her loosely tied hair sway forward, covering her face. The woman had magnetic eyes. She emanated energy like a halo.

Angad felt embarrassed. However, he managed to say - Hi! and introduced himself. "I know, I had a long chat with Raghu. He mentioned you," she said and smiled naughtily. "Seems like Raghu has already filled her mind about me," thought Angad. Maybe he had told this woman about his illicit bond with Yamini. If so, she would judge him as an unbecoming gentleman. Angad was clueless. He wanted to move on, showing no interest in continuing a dialogue with her. She smiled at him as he continued to climb with his eyes set on her. She stood there, scanning him all over until he disappeared. Away from her prying eyes, he relaxed.

He thought of some similarity between Yamini Peter and this new imposing personality who had moved into flat number 203. In contrast, Yamini was soft, smooth and calm. This lady appeared rigid from her looks.

Entering his flat, Angad relaxed. He felt

disappointed at the way he had behaved earlier. Though the lady was friendly, Angad had not reciprocated in the same tone. "I must apologise to her later for being impolite," he decided.

Some random issues started popping up in the advertising agency. A few members quit. The workload increased. Most assignments never met deadlines, like the caption for a newly launched noodle or the copy for a grocery delivery service. Angad had started the job with no experience. Faking up and some presentation skills had landed him the job. Copywriting was not as charming a job as it was made out to be. Writing to fulfil someone's requirement is termed creativity.

For a few days, he had been contemplating quitting. It was relatively easy. His conscience did not accept the idea. That too, when the company was not doing well. "Even if I quit, I will do so after completing my assignments," thought Angad.

It was a bold decision to put himself in complete isolation and work twelve to fourteen hours a day to complete his work. He finished many assignments. Some got rejected, but most got accepted. About three weeks later, he had a firm grip on what he was doing. His seniors applauded the efforts and the results. Angad got reasonable control on the job.

Angad was waiting for a chance to meet Anuradha. Due to his work regime, he did not see anyone in the apartment, the corridor or the staircase when he left home early and returned late at night. Perhaps Anuradha too was staying and working elsewhere, with a tight work schedule like mine, he reasoned.

Then, out of nowhere, Angad stepped out of his flat and met Anuradha face-to-face. She looked straight out of a Ravi Varma's portrait. With her distinctive unmissable personality, she was locking her house to leave for her job. The untameable authoritarian smiled and looked deep into his eyes.

Angad started to feel a bit uneasy. She looked as if she was scanning a person from top to bottom. Her uniform had the logo of the Mission Hospital. She was working for the hospital. Her nametag pinned to her saree announced that she was an Administrative Officer there. Probably, she was authoritative because of her professional requirement which demanded one to have a watchful eye. "We are our characters; we are known for the way we are. Our thoughts shape our physique," Angad contemplated.

Both of them smiled and greeted each other at the same time. Anuradha kept smiling. She spoke as if reciting a poem. They climbed down the staircase together. She kept talking to him and walked ahead, prompting Angad to follow her.

The regular vegetable vendor with his salt and pepper beard called out the names of his merchandise, drowning Anuradha's voice. Angad looked at the vendor's cart. The vendor shouted out the names of the vegetables as if reciting a nursery rhyme unaware, as usual, whether he was carrying all the vegetables he named or not.

The uneven footpath and passers-by on the busy Hospital Street made it difficult for them to walk together. Angad struggled to keep pace with Anuradha. They both reached the hospital gate, and Angad continued to follow her in a trance. When the guard at the gate saluted Anuradha, Angad realised how lost was he. He had followed her despite knowing he had to take a different route. Angad stood there watching Anuradha walk towards the hospital building, greeting her staff. She did not notice that Angad wasn't accompanying her anymore. He walked towards his office to write a few copies that thousands would read later.

Anuradha was a spinster from Mumbai and was new to the city. She stayed alone. After a few meetings in the building corridor, Angad had the feeling that Anuradha knew that the previous occupant of the flat had vacated after a rumoured illicit bond between the married woman and Angad. The entire apartment gossiped behind Angad's back.

A crow settled close to Angad. It shook its shiny bill, swivelling its head from left to right. Carefully looking around, it picked a few grains without fearing Angad's presence. Its eyes glowed.

"Even the crow's mind must be continuously producing numerous thoughts like a human. Do these birds smile or laugh? Maybe, they do. Perhaps, humans cannot perceive the way they laugh or smile," pondered Angad. A myna kept hitting the glass shutter with its beak. This one came almost daily, hitting the glass shutter persistently.

Anuradha, despite the usual greetings, maintained a distance from him. The rumours in the corridor painted Angad to be a bad sort. "Birds of a feather flock together." "Did she judge me?" such thoughts disturbed Angad.

This society had a set of unprinted rules, and people voluntarily accepted them. Everyone makes an opinion. It comes impulsively.

Angad's mother called him regularly. She sounded fine but insisted on his return. It was the first time since he had moved to the city that she sternly asked him to return. After talking for a while, she started weeping uncontrollably. Had the world she built around her suddenly collapsed?

She was unable to control her emotions. The loneliness was everywhere. She had started fine. Then as she continued to talk, she could not bear the loneliness anymore. And she was unable to fake the presence of her dearly departed husband any longer. Angad got an idea. He wanted to invite his mother to the city and show her the Hospital Street. But the thought remained unspoken as she cut the call short.

The veins of the leaves were visible under the sun as they swayed in tandem with the breeze. A well-organised army of ants marched on the Gulmohar trunk while a crowd of humans moved helter-skelter in the street below, lost in thoughts for creating a better tomorrow.

Angad stood watching the Hospital Street aimlessly. The intoxicating smell of fresh *sambar* from Anand Bhawan enveloped the entire street. It made people stop, smile and inhale. The flavour produced by the combination of asafoetida, lentils and several other spices covered the length and breadth of the street, inviting people to the restaurant.

An ambulance siren reverberated through the street. Vehicles and the crowd parted, giving way to the ambulance. Tension gripped the hospital for a while, a routine by now. People cried and shouted. Maybe Anuradha, with her dedicated staff, was trying to control the crowd and address them.

The mob-like gathering swelled in a short time. It seemed like a political leader or a celebrity had arrived as a patient. A team of men and women in police uniform arrived in jeeps wielding their lathis, prompting the crowd to disperse. The ambulance returned with a shrill siren. People ran behind it. In minutes, the crowd's density decreased, and the scene was ready for something else.

Angad's mother called. She sounded strange and seemed to worry a lot. For all these years, she had someone close to her for everything. Now that there was a vacuum in her life, she found it unable to bear. She pleaded Angad to return. Angad's idea to bring her to the city was rejected immediately. Many days passed by. His mother's distress calls and pleas had influenced Angad, who then decided to return.

Anuradha shunned Angad, and the initial enthusiasm she expressed eroded. Many a time, Angad had stood outside the flat number 203, resisting the urge to meet her. It was not Anuradha who attracted him. Anyone who stayed in flat number 203; draped in black and red saree, would draw Angad's attention as an imprint left by Yamini. He made many failed attempts to meet her at the hospital.

Angad's work schedule did not match hers as she worked extra hours. Despite clashing working hours and busy schedules, they did meet a few times. Anuradha's workload kept her in the hospital for long hours, and she liked caring for people. Angad was happy with the thought that she had not deliberately distanced herself from him. Still, the overwhelming friendliness shown during the first few meetings was missing. The more Angad tried to get closer to her, the more she distanced herself, or maybe, he just felt that way.

Angad's thoughts hovered around Anuradha.

In his thoughts, he dressed her up in a black silk blouse and draped her in a shining blood-red saree. He painted her meticulously to turn her into another Yamini. He combed her fragrant black hair, parted it in the middle and put them through a hairband. He placed a red *bindi* on her forehead. She looked like a goddess. He twirled her eyelashes and drew the eyebrows extending to the temple. Her eyes, now even brighter, pointed at him. He felt her nose, lip, chin and neck. He created Yamini out of Anuradha. Yet, she was different from Yamini. Yamini was soft and charming. Anuradha was strong and dominating.

His mother kept on calling him frequently. Whenever she called, she appeared to be a different person. Sometimes, she spoke too much and, at times, too little. Sometimes, she said irrelevant things. She was changing, but her newness was inconsistent.

Angad's obsession with Anuradha was growing. There was no moment left when Angad had not visualised Anuradha's presence. He had learnt the projection technique from his mother. Anuradha came to him, touched him, caressed him and tickled every tiny cell in him, sending him into a tease.

Days passed. Raghu came and left for his official work. Raghu's life was captivated by accounting books; his life was all about tallying accounts and matching digits. Everyone exists in minuteness— like being confined in a pond and never moving in or out of it.

A few satisfying copies were written and accepted by the management—a few lines for a new spice brand. Angad was unsure, but some thoughts and ideas that cropped in from somewhere helped. The agency was doubly happy when the client appreciated the catchy and attractive phrases he wrote. Angad was clueless about how it all fits together.

His feelings for Anuradha were at a peak. He constantly thought of her and felt her presence in everything around him. He did not have to think about her deliberately. It came naturally. He could hold her thoughts for hours, projecting her presence, helping the law of attraction work.

One fine evening, when Angad was spending time with the ants and other creatures around in the harmony of nature, the doorbell rang. With a calm mind, he went to open the door. It was Anuradha, smiling as if a thousand suns were glittering; her robe with a bright red that was close to what he had imagined. Her hair, the *bindi* on her forehead, her eyebrows trespassing the temple and beyond, and other features were more or less what he had visualised. Angad was not surprised, for he knew he was trying to attract her through his constant thoughts. While projecting her in his mind, he was deliberately scripting it into his life. Angad worked so intensely to attract her towards himself. And when he worked, the world worked.

Angad guided her through the living room and shared the sit-out area with her. She was more than amused when she heard about Angad's incredible connection with all the little creatures around him. Angad guided her into his world of visualisation, free from the gravity of the present, liberated to a self-created world. She too found it interesting. A self-exploration for her—a novel feeling. Visualise and achieve in the same manner an ad agency visualises a print advertisement or an executive in an agency visualises the end result long before it is printed.

Anuradha, although reluctantly, embarked on a journey with Angad. Angad felt safe in Anuradha's intense company and submitted to her authority.

Everything could be kept captive and controlled, but not the mind. The mind wanders to newer areas. It wanders to create a new tomorrow.

Anuradha slowly released her hand held tightly by Angad. She shook it in relief. Nothing developed between them. It remained a non-committed friendship and nothing more. Angad had not sought anything more. He had just created her everywhere around him and left it there.

Anuradha's mind had already visualised an

even stronger and safer hands of her colleague in the hospital. Angad had no idea how close she was to Dr. Prakash. He did not know that a set of desires stronger than what he had created was working on the other end.

That development did not cause any resentment in Angad. He coolly accepted it. He once again withdrew himself and went back to the world of stakeholders.

CHAPTER ELEVEN

Amma arrived unannounced. This visit was a part of her act of being bold. It was probably the first time she stepped out alone on an out-station trip.

Anuradha's perfume in his room sowed the seeds of doubt in her mind. She saw a potential daughter-in-law in her. A strong woman who walked, moved, talked and breathed like a leader all the time. Perhaps, she projected a tough life ahead under the strict control of her would-be daughter-in-law.

Anuradha was a few years older than Angad. On knowing this, his mother mentioned that even if Angad wanted to marry her, it would be without her blessings. She wanted a daughter-in-law who was younger than her son, as was the traditional practice.

Mother had already expressed her displeasure about his friendship with Anuradha. Angad cleared her doubts, saying that there was nothing between the two, but he enjoyed her company. He, too, would not be comfortable with her authoritative character, he added. Angad told his mother all that he knew about Anuradha and her job at the hospital. She was relieved when Angad repeatedly told her that he had no plans to propose to her for marriage.

Mother is an emotion. A force that captivates everything around. Her presence makes any place more than just a building with brick and mortar. She puts everything in perfect order. The kitchen became an active place. Her presence helped Anuradha distance herself from Angad.

His mother kept the house clean and tidy, much to his delight. Her presence around gave him freedom and liberated Angad's creativity level. He could quickly write a few copies, and the management was happy with his improved copywriting. Perhaps, one's creativity increases when the surrounding is calm and peaceful.

Amidst all these, his mother would remind him of the need to return home. She often talked of how she would not be comfortable anywhere else but in her own home. Her heart was there because that was where she felt the presence of her departed husband.

Angad was indecisive. However, he, too, felt that life at the Hospital Street was becoming increasingly dull. He saw no point in continuing with his present job. He did not think along the lines of making a career out of it. It was a temporary arrangement to make ends meet. Beyond that, it was nothing more. If there's a lack of passion for what one does, the job becomes a mechanical activity. It becomes lifeless.

Angad decided to bid goodbye to his temporary

profession. The agency, too, was going through a rough time as there was no more funding from investors.

Dropping the leather bag on the settee, he announced quitting his job to his mother. She smiled. Hiding her happiness, she headed straight to the kitchen to prepare some snacks for him.

He had taken this decision reluctantly and wanted a second opinion from someone close to him. He had no one to turn to. Raghu was not around, and Anuradha, though close by, had moved away from him. It dawned upon him that he did not have anyone around him to seek support from, someone to lean on, or someone to confide in. "All along, my inner consciousness has only been my friend. Maybe I don't need a friend. I have many characters inside me. And all the characters are my friends," felt Angad. "It is senseless to have friends to discuss worldly matters or seek support on earthly issues as long as one feels connected with every being around." "Every morning, I get up and start talking to myself. I can trust the person in me. He keeps my secrets, and listens to my foolish ideas;" he thought to himself.

Raghu dropped in without any notice and was surprised when Angad's mother opened the door. He had met her last when Angad and his mother had attended his wedding a few years ago. He was pleasantly surprised to see the apartment tidy. He entered his house like a guest.

Raghu was uncomfortable in such a tidy place; he missed the untidiness of his flat. The kitchen looked like it had been turned into an entirely new one. Raghu's own room, which Angad's mother seldom entered, was the only place where he could find some respite and felt his own.

Angad's mother remained busy during the weekend, cooking for both of them. Those days, Angad skipped his regular interactive sessions on the balcony with the other stakeholders of the earth. Raghu too missed his weekend drinking sessions as *Amma* was around.

Amma announced her plans to return home and asked Angad to come along. She underlined the fact that since he had quit his job, there was no point in him continuing to stay there.

It was then that Raghu got to know that Angad had resigned. When Raghu asked for the reason behind his decision, Angad struggled for an answer, as he himself wasn't convinced of his reasons.

The next day, mother packed her bags. She had now become independent. "I had underestimated my mother all these years," thought Angad. At the same time, he felt proud of her. "People lean onto others and become dependent on them. However, when they find no one around them. They learn to stand on their own. This had happened in my mother's case;" reasoned Angad.

She walked into the room and announced that she had planned to leave the next day and wanted Angad to join her. "Pack your bags, Angad, or shall I do the needful?" Was his mother dictating terms to him? He thought that she was not giving him a choice for a second.

Raghu sat on the edge of the settee as a mute spectator. "When I came here, I travelled in an unreserved compartment; it was very crowded;" mother complained lowly. "This time around, you reserve seats on a train. A bus is also fine," saying that she moved to the kitchen.

Squeezing the synthetic cover of the settee, Raghu tried to change the topic. What were Angad's career plans? To Raghu's question, mother replied from the kitchen, which neither could hear. While Raghu and Angad chatted over an uncertain career ahead, the mother's responses drowned in the utensils clattering.

They both chatted until sunset. Raghu wanted to catch the evening bus to Hubli to report to the local office the following day. He would be drowned in government expense files and ledgers for quite some time. He would dive into the ocean of expenditure registers and files to bring up the pearls of misappropriation. To the best of his knowledge, Raghu was an honest person, which meant that no officer would be able to escape any wayward expenses.

Raghu always struggled to balance his income with his growing expenditure despite a well-paid job. When he spoke, he would mention the lack of money most of the time. He was always pessimistic about finance.

"He constantly thinks about the absence of richness and attracts the lack of it. Why can't he think of its abundance and attract abundance? Or why can't he be satisfied with what he has? Some people do not understand the process of life at all," Angad pitied him. Feeling content with what had come naturally to Angad, not by practice or force. Scarcity is invited, it is created. People always complain about the lack of something. They never acknowledge abundance. If the whole world thought of the abundance of money, the world would be so rich.

Raghu left late in the evening. He had asked Angad to hide the keys at a particular spot near the window sill just in case Angad left before he returned from Hubli.

Mother pestered him regularly about his plans to return. It looked like she would not leave the place without Angad. She unpacked her luggage and waited for him to make up his mind once and for all.

Anuradha and *Amma* formed a connection. When Anuradha was home, his mother would barge in and hang around for hours. They had a harmonious relationship. His mother would have proposed an alliance for Angad if only the girl had not been older than him.

He planned a return from the city as his mother would not budge without him. And he wanted to spend time with his mother rather than be alone on the balcony.

That evening, on the balcony, his mother sat close to Angad; sipping a steaming cup of tea. Patting him on his knee while holding the tea in the other, she said: "Let us leave in a few days." Angad was ready to follow her and put himself under her wing.

The creatures moved about as usual. They lived in a world created by them. We live in a world created by us. Angad watched the tiny creatures crawling on the parapet. Just like us humans, these creatures could also have names, families, friends, and social obligations. Our world and their worlds are connected. We call them creatures or animals, while we humans label ourselves as higher beings.

Some people started gathering a few feet away from the cobbler's shop. When people parted, he spotted a large polythene banner covering the hedge. Shoes were being sold at factory prices. The next day while walking down the street, Angad met the cobbler and checked about the new shoe vendor he had seen the previous day. The happy cobbler had a different tale to tell altogether. His son had managed to get some good quality shoes from a wholesale vendor. He put up a new brand name and showcased them as if on sale at factory prices. With a made-up fashionable European brand name, limited period and low price, the boy had managed to sell everything in a few hours. The delight on the face of the shoemaker was evident when he said -- "My son seems to know the tricks, and he is smart, sir." The proud parent happily continued, "He said he would make it big in the footwear business one day. He will do it because he earned in a day what I would have earned in three months." His face was glowing with happiness. "Looks a big footwear businessman is in the making with deal-breaking ideas," thought Angad.

The train was almost full. Both mother and son settled down in their berths. Angad made sure that his mother was comfortable in the lower berth. Trying to sleep in the middle berth was futile; he could hardly catch a wink.

A mother and her child were struggling to share the lower birth on the other side. The child often cried, expressing her discomfort. When the child started bawling, Angad's mother gave some advice to the young mother, and within minutes, the child stopped crying. We seldom understand the captivating power of mothers.

Slowly, the train moved out of the station.

The doors were shut, and the windows shutters were lowered. The sound of the engine drowned the cacophony of sellers.

He covered himself in the freshly washed cotton bedsheet his mother had given him when he occupied the berth. It smelt of Melastoma flowers. Someone in the upper birth started snoring. The conductor in his usual uniform came in and verified everyone before leaving for the next coupe.

The train moved to a rhythm. It was a rhythm that is a part and parcel of most of the middle-class people of India. As the night progressed, lights were turned off one after the other, and only a narrow shaft of light near the lavatory remained.

An older man cautiously walked down the aisle, making his way towards the toilet. The locomotive slowed down for some time and the older man returned to his berth, checking all the coupes en route. When half of the world was sleeping in the darkness of the night, Angad faked a deep sleep covering his face with the fresh cotton sheet that smelt of his mother.

The bright morning sunlight hit Angad in the face through the window grills, forcing his eyes to open. They had arrived home in the wee hours and he hit his dusty bed straightaway and drifted into a sound slumber. He looked at the clock. It was nine.

Amma was talking to someone. He could not

make out who the person was. It sounded like she got someone to clean the house. A few weeks of leaving it unused had made it dusty and covered in cobwebs. Angad stretched, rubbed his sleepy eyes and woke up. He smiled at his mother and picked up a ceiling duster to join her in cleaning their home. "Leave it. Go and have your breakfast. We will finish cleaning the hall and join you," said his mother.

The person assisting his mother was a worker from the neighbourhood. For any casual work, his mother always asked her for help. In her fifties or so, the woman greeted Angad pleasantly and soon wanted to know what he had been up to. Women are always curious about men's careers. Angad managed to evade a direct answer, trying to confuse the woman. Taking a cue from what Angad said, she continued her conversation with his mother, and the topic moved to a different one.

Mother flung the broom on the floor and asked him to follow her to the dining area. She invited the lady to have breakfast, too. However, the lady moved to the veranda and continued to dust the seating area.

He savoured the spicy, tangy *rava upma* that had a fresh aroma of curry leaves. It reminded him of the Hospital Street and Ananda Bhavan. His mother, too ate, shuffling between the kitchen platform and the dining table as she prepared tea as well. When the tea was about to boil over, she rushed to turn off the stove.

The lady resumed cleaning the hall, asking for some cloth to dust the furniture. "Angad, I plan to visit Satish sometime next week;" mother said with a grin. "You can join me too. It has been a while since I last visited him."

Satish was his mother's younger brother who worked in the police department in Mercara, a hill town. His wife taught in a local school there. To be able to live with her, his uncle had managed to avoid transfers to other places. He had worked away from the town only once or twice in his entire career. But that came at a price. He had forgone promotions.

"I will tell you later, *Amma*;" said Angad and went to his room. "Stay here until we dust and clean your room," said *Amma*.

It was a four-hour journey to Mercara. *Amma* could manage alone, he thought. She had had a minor tiff with her brother on a trivial issue at a family gathering. His uncle, the policeman, had spoken bluntly to his older sister, which hurt her no end. Since then, they have been estranged.

The siblings often fought over trivial issues. However, the tension between the two would not last long. The tiff had put off her occasional trips to Mercara. But it was not a feeling that lasted long.

Angad's childhood summers were always spent

in their traditional palatial house at Mercara, where his grandparents lived until they passed away. Those summer days were full of nostalgia and were unforgettable. Angad would get dropped off at his mother's ancestral home on the first day of his holidays and spend nearly two months there with his cousins.

The world there was different from here. Or maybe the feeling was different—the brilliant dark green pastures with a thick grove. The friendly neighbourhood offered a lot.

His cousin Sunil knew the terrain like the back of his hand. Trekking with him was always fun. Angad and Sunil would lie on their backs on massive boulders on the hillock until Grandma came calling.

Remembering Grandma, Angad's taste buds began to tingle. When returning after a tiring football game in the semi-dry paddy fields around the hillocks, she would welcome them with tangy buttermilk.

He glided through those unforgettable memories until his mother asked him to leave the room. He yearned to be back again in the valley.

"*Amma*, I will join you."

She lifted her head as if on cue and looked at Angad, surprised at the timing of his response. Drops of sweat ran down her face as she wiped it with her *pallu*.

The following Sunday, Angad and his mother set out early in the morning for the hills. *Amma* had called up her brother and asked him to pick her up from the bus terminus.

Briefly after her husband's death, she had weakened. But then, somehow, she regained her confidence. She was reborn as a new person, a positive person —a person who suddenly started believing in manifesting through positive thinking. However, her previous unsure self would pop up off and on.

"A son of my age should be supporting his mother. Here I am living under her shadow," thought Angad.

Angad put his hand over his mother's hand and leaned a bit over her shoulder in an attempt to relax in the bus that was scaling up the mountainous terrain. *Amma* held him close.

"What rule of nature makes a person like me be born to such a wonderful human being?" Angad contemplated. The hilly terrain was cold and misty and offered an incredible ambience. Angad drifted into his past.

CHAPTER TWELVE

Her brother was waiting for her arrival in his worn-out jeep at the bus stop. There he stood, looking courteous and respectful towards his elder sister. Angad felt that his uncle was overdoing it a bit.

After a period of friction between the siblings, the patch-up happened after Angad's father's death. Ever since then, the brother and his sister had stayed in touch. However, Angad's connection with his uncle was limited to the summer holidays. Uncle looked tough. He was stout with a broad chest and had a sharp face with a black pointed moustache. One look at him, and anyone could make out from his appearance that he was either in the police or in the army.

Uncle kept himself busy all the time by doing something or the other. Should one not find him on duty at the police station, he would be in the nearby fields looking after trees. If he had not been a policeman, he would have been a farmer. Not any ordinary farmer but a gifted one who had made a fortune because of his talent in alternate ways of farming. He also ran a retail outlet for agricultural inputs that was opened or closed depending on his convenience. His wife was his perfect partner. She, too, accompanied him to help in his farm work. In her case, if she was not busy teaching her students at school, she would be with her husband in their small yet very fertile land.

Uncle helped his sister sit in the front seat of the jeep. He helped her place her legs properly. He then asked Angad to join them in the front row as well. With all three of them packed in the jeep, Uncle drove with great skill through the narrow lanes invaded by branches of coffee plants leading to the house where he and *Amma* had grown up.

Scaling the hillock, he stopped his jeep right in front of a temple, a few meters off the road with a narrow, stone-paved entrance. Jumping out of the vehicle, he asked them to follow. The way Uncle asked them to follow, Angad had a feeling that the temple was their final destination. Angad alighted from the jeep followed by *Amma*. She followed her brother while Angad stayed back, enjoying the view of the vast coffee estate that belonged to some Mumbai corporate. Within minutes, both of them returned. Uncle Satish smiled at Angad and turned to his sister to check if he was still an atheist. Mother commented teasingly, "He is still an ignorant boy" Uncle continued his adventurous driving along the bank of the majestic Bhavli River shimmering in the sunlight, a jewel in the crown of Mercara.

The jeep halted in front of the new house, reconstructed precisely at the same site where the old one stood. Most memories faded with the demolition of the ancestral house. The sense of belonging had gone. On hearing the clanging of the jeep, Angad's aunt came rushing out. She was expecting them and gave due regard to her husband's elder sister by welcoming them traditionally into the house. Angad watched his mother change into an older person who needed care.

The aroma of ripe oranges and coffee permeated the air. A grove surrounded the house, no small thanks to the hard work put in by his uncle and aunt.

After placing their luggage near the settee in the living room, Uncle Satish pulled off his shirt and flung it to a corner. It revealed the biceps that he had gained working in the field. He was probably preparing himself to use the spade in the grove. Foreseeing this, Angad's aunt said something that prompted him to retire to the settee and sit next to his sister.

Though it was a newly built house, it looked more like an old storehouse with coconuts, areca nuts, coffee beans, agricultural equipment, and tools kept helter-skelter.

Having seen so many poor farmers, Angad wondered at the abundance of crops here. Suddenly his uncle jumped out of the settee, picked up a sickle and then disappeared for a while. In the middle of her chat with her sister-in-law, his aunt made a sarcastic comment about her husband's unstoppable passion for work when she saw him going out with the sickle. Uncle reappeared with a few tender coconuts. He asked his wife not to prepare coffee and to give his sister fresh coconut water instead. She appreciated his thoughtful gesture. Her long shiny hair swayed when she moved, covering her like a shawl.

Aunt's prying mind now moved its attention to Angad. She expressed her concern about him being jobless, indirectly aiming at her nephew's decreasing chances of a good marriage. She threw a barrage of questions to know the actual reason behind him leaving his bank job. Angad's mother tried to explain without blaming him for his decision to quit. However, she was not convinced. She glared at Angad. Angad was not bothered. He was enjoying his childhood summer memories.

Uncle chopped off the tips of the tender coconuts with one sharp move of the sickle. He handed out the coconuts to each one, beginning with his sister. Either it came naturally to him, or he was trying to please the elderly.

A large photo frame of their son adorned the white wall. Angad's childhood companion, his cousin's portrait in a well-decorated army uniform. Of late, Angad and Sunil had hardly connected, maybe once in several months. He had called Angad from Chandigarh when he heard of Angad's father's demise. It was not a deliberate choice. Somehow, people adapt to certain daily chores and do not think beyond the routine.

Amma's eyes settled on the portrait and she started enquiring about Sunil and his career. Aunt turned highly vocal about her son's adventurous career. Angad started getting uncomfortable. The status of one's employment suddenly disqualified him as being fit for society. It robbed him of all other qualities.

While leaving home, his mother had mentioned spending three to four days here. However, the way things developed, it looked like the stay could be longer. Angad was happy to see his mother enjoying little things in her brother's house as if she was a permanent resident there.

More than a retired policeman, his uncle was a full-time farmer and a supplier for the area. It was a pleasant surprise to see someone doing well in farming. His uncle did something most farmers did not. He did it as a business.

Angad's mother also owned a piece of land here, which his uncle took care of. Uncle settled an old farm income account with his sister giving her bundles of cash rolled and tied with rubber bands. Handing each wad, he named the harvest against which it was received. She accepted the money after some initial resistance.

Angad had a meet-up with his childhood summer friends. Some were doing well, while others were struggling to make ends meet. Life seemed to be a constant struggle for making money, be it for survival or pride.

After a week, *Amma* decided to return and ordered Angad to join. Angad did what he was asked to do. In a few interactions with his uncle, Angad concluded that inside a stout body; there lived a pious and saintly man. Angad paid heed to whatever his uncle said to him while walking on the terrace, gazing into the unknown world of the stars.

Continuing to gaze at the stars in the uncharted world, his uncle talked about his belief in the local deity, a complete submission without questioning. He would have believed in any god or deity. For him, his unchallenged belief was to save himself from thoughts that haunted him. If his uncle did not anchor his mind on something or someone, it would wander elsewhere; around numerous things, producing unwanted thoughts.

Belief helps. Even not believing is also a kind of belief. Uncle sounded like a preacher. "Angad, what you believed yesterday is happening today, and what you believe right now will happen tomorrow. Belief is the root of everything that is happening. Believe firmly and unquestionably, and it will happen." He added saying, "It is not that the deity makes it happen. It is your belief that makes it happen. The deity helps you believe it because we hardly can believe it ourselves."

Uncle went on talking. Angad grasped a little that he found fascinating. "The whole world is what we perceive it as and what we call or name it," Uncle paused for a moment and then continued, "Are you listening to me?"

"Yes, Uncle," Angad responded quickly.

When he moved closer to his uncle, he found him lost in his thoughts, and he smelt some smooth, smoky drink from him. Earlier that evening, Angad had seen his uncle inhale a drink several times before tasting it. He had a vast, ancient traditional-designed wooden cupboard that contained several liquor bottles. He was probably a connoisseur. Sometimes, he 'ate' the drink, making some noises rather than drinking it. He seemed to focus and enjoy every bit of what he did.

When Angad was young, his uncle appeared friendly but did not talk much. He had always appeared as a rugged, weathered policeman with a somewhat ruffian appearance. There were moments of pride when he used to stand at the market junction in his uniform, wielding a lathi, being in charge of the entire area. He would sternly warn encroachers and unruly people while twirling his moustache.

Whenever in town, Angad never lost an

opportunity to walk up to his uncle to show people that the most powerful person at the crossroads was easily accessible to him. The same strong man, after retirement, turned pious and god-fearing. He kept himself busy all the time. He got up early, wore a greyed bath towel on his head, carried a long bamboo stick, and set out to supervise his farms. A *lathi* was his lifelong companion, from being a policeman to working on the farm. His day started with a *lathi*.

A long walk with multiple purposes! A few minutes of chit-chat with everyone on the way was a must – casual, shallow talks, but as necessary as oxygen. It refreshed him. He advised people, not to use hazardous pesticides or how to use them wisely. As a nature lover, he hated the usage of chemical pesticides on farm produces. He advocated the use of natural remedies for pests and disease control in the field. He encouraged people to do low-budget farming; spending minimum and reaping maximum seemed to be his policy. Maybe, that was the reason for his abundance.

Like Angad, he too interacted with his plants and cows. He believed that the plants understood what he said. He even felt that the plants leaned towards him, lending their ears whenever he communicated with them. Uncle waited for their responses. He touched, caressed and kissed them.

Uncle usually returned in an hour or so to

savour the steaming tea in the copper pot. Sitting on the cold veranda, he slurped on his cup of tea, and that was the only way he enjoyed nearly half a litre of aromatic tea. This sage seemed to enjoy every little thing he did. One could learn how to read a newspaper from him. If he were not in a hurry to return to the farm, he would read the day's newspaper from top to bottom loudly. He read every news item with relevant theatrical expressions. He made a lot of noise, savouring each bit of news like it were a spicy pickle. It was fun to watch him read. He recreated some of the news as an audio drama by changing his tone and playing the story for everyone to hear.

Angad heard his aunt quip as to how she doesn't need to read the newspaper since his uncle read it so loudly that everyone, including the neighbours, was updated daily. People who lived close by understood his passion.

Uncle Satish ate a substantial breakfast. He ate as much as he could, enjoying every bite to the hilt. His massive breakfast was followed by nearly half a litre of tea with extra sugar.

It was only now that Angad had started to observe and understand his uncle. For his uncle, each activity was a part of his prayer. He was deliberately getting involved in everything he did so that his mind was firmly anchored.

Angad's respect for his uncle doubled. He

looked up to him as a master and adored him for his noble thoughts. He did a lot of things between his breakfast and lunch. He spoke less, spoke meaningfully and did something or the other that was productive.

The shocking and tragic experience with Narendra Prasad had tainted Angad's attitude towards farming. But his uncle's steady wealth created from farming reversed his views completely. Uncle farmed with complete dedication. He loved everything on the farm; he never complained. He believed that if he cursed the rain when it rained too much, it would vanish for good. And he knew when he condemned the sun; there wouldn't be sun for days on end.

For lunch, he sat on the veranda cross-legged as shining droplets of sweat dripped from his hairy chest. He would wolf down a portion of rice, curry and his favourite, a freshly caught fish from the Bhavli River brought by his childhood friend as a token of their friendship. He would relish every morsel of food. He ate noisily. It was because he enjoyed it to the fullest like he did everything else. That was his way of doing anything. By now, uncle was turning into a subject for Angad to fathom. Angad observed his every action and thought.

He had an impeccably fit physique with short, uneven grey hair and a hairy chest. The white loincloth around his waist had gained the smell and colour of the fresh earth.

Angad was not sure if he wanted to follow his uncle's lifestyle. At the outset, his uncle's behaviour looked like any other person around him. However, the way uncle diligently finished his routine chores seemed like he was in love with everything he did.

"At times, we do not see the good souls close to us but search for them elsewhere," felt Angad. It was the same when it came to his uncle. He was an enlightened soul. Angad gave a place of prominence to his uncle in his heart and worshipped him silently.

In the evening, his uncle fixed a large peg to drink on the veranda, massaging himself with some herbal oil. This routine generally lasted an hour. Angad had always connected the smell of that particular oil with his uncle, and he had never smelt it anywhere or on anyone before or after.

The self-massage and drink would finish around the same time. It was followed by a quick shower and an even quicker dinner. The dinner was a handful of rice with a spoonful of curry. Thus, he innately practised what seemed a healthy food intake.

For everything his uncle did, the ardent admirer in Angad found something divine in it. Unnoticeably, Angad was getting influenced by his uncle, and he started viewing life from a different standpoint.

Days passed by. Leaning on his mother's shoulder, Angad returned home. The rickety old bus made its way along green paddy fields in sharp contrast to the shining golden panicles across the vast land which offered a sense of wealth. *Amma* was a bit uncomfortable with his head over her shoulder. The constant wabbling of the bus didn't help either, but she didn't complain.

Angad was pondering over what his uncle taught him on those tranquil evenings. He looked at himself in a new light. He felt as if his existence was that of mere flesh and bones. He felt himself like an object on the resin-upholstered seat of the bus. His mind was slowly opening up to a different realm. "What is this existence?" he wondered.

There were nearly three dozen bundles of flesh and bones in that metal box. In contrast, Angad was in another dimension altogether.

The bus jolted to a sudden stop. A majestic serpent was crossing the road. The driver let the snake take its own sweet time. A few people stood up from their seats to take in the sight. Some made senseless comments. Some remembered their gods. Others dropped their jaws in awe. The bus moved along. Though Angad moved along with it, his brain was processing what his uncle told him.

Uncle's version of life was designed in such a

way that no man would ever find peace. Even if someone achieved harmony, the same peace would become a source of distress. That is the way we were created. Angad viewed everyone on the bus as machines made up of flesh and bones. Tools to produce continuous thoughts. Amidst dozens of passengers, Angad felt alone.

The bus halted near a food hub. Angad's mother lifted her shoulder to wake him up. He raised his head and found himself in yet another new dimension. Others woke up and jumped out of the bus. One by one, many buses continued to arrive and halt at the food hub, creating a crowd. The counters were doing brisk business; some takeaways, while most offered food on their tables. Some attendants were loudly repeating orders for the kitchen staff to hear. Crowds made Angad uneasy.

Another bus arrived. Young children disembarked, chatting loudly like a flock of birds. They came out in a queue like a herd of domesticated animals, under the watchful eyes of a grim-faced, spectacled elderly lady. There was a cloth banner tied in the front of the bus. The school's name was one of those that Angad regularly saw at the Hospital Street junction. A few food hub staff rushed to guide the children to a corner. Perhaps, they had made some prior booking. The pleasant-faced little girls and boys marched into the restaurant in a straight line.

Angad's bus driver started honking for the passengers to return. He started the engine and accelerated it intermittently, prompting the passengers to return to the bus. After all the passengers were seated, the driver's assistant walked through the aisle, re-checking the occupants. He gave the go-ahead signal to the driver. The driver honked one last time for no reason and pulled his vehicle onto the highway. He scared the crows that were pecking on heaps of food waste negligently left by the roadside. As the bus moved on, the crows returned to the pile of garbage. The fragrance of fresh jasmine flowers hung in the air. Most passengers were now chattering after the rejuvenating stop.

As the bus rolled on, Angad dived into the memories of the time spent with his uncle. He introspected every little thing that his uncle had said. One evening, his uncle was taking a stroll in his front yard, post his usual ration of drinks. In the dim light from the veranda, uncle's face looked thoughtful. In the growing evening cold, he seemed not to be 'present' there but in the future. Uncle mumbled about the numerous changes that would take place in the same place. He said that all the people here now would pass away into another world. The plants, bushes and shrubs would cease to exist. A few more years down the line, even the house would disappear, making space for a new one. "This endless expanse remains as it is and is timeless. Or, it may change; who knows?" His visualisation scared Angad. His uncle kept talking, perhaps the effects of alcohol helped him delve deep. Later, after a shower and then dinner, they hit the sack.

Back on the bus, newer thoughts carried Angad away. He floated, lost in the thoughts induced by his uncle. Angad looked at his mother, fast asleep on the passenger seat, leaning over the backrest, with her head positioned in a relaxed mode. "This wonderful, towering woman who gave birth to me and raised and nurtured me will be lost someday." The space she occupied on this earth now will be empty.

Feeling her deep breath closely and knowing that he could lose her one day, he felt a strain of current going down his spine. Angad leaned over her like a little child, waking her up. "Are you okay?" she asked him, placing her cold palm over his forehead to check his temperature.

Angad grew anxious to experience every moment. "Why do I exist? Where did I start this life? Where and when will it end? What moves all these ahead?" thinking about all these questions, he closed his eyes.

Angad did not answer his mother. Instead, he moved even closer to her. He feared losing her. He was worried about an unexpected 'next' moment. He lost his peace of mind.

The bus rumbled on, moving over a speed breaker. Everyone was rattled. People complained because something unexpected had happened. People were designed to expect what was routine and seamless; the wheel over the speed breaker had shattered their perfect design. Angad straightened himself.

"Why are you so silent?" his concerned mother asked him.

CHAPTER THIRTEEN

The veranda was covered in dust and dry leaves that had accumulated over more than a week. Nature was slowly taking over as the mother and her son were not disturbing it. A mix of soil, twigs and feathers were scattered all over. Perhaps some birds were trying to build a nest. Now the presence of the mother and her son would put an end to it.

Angad's mother had her work cut out for the rest of the day. She managed to get her regular maid and started cleaning the house. Sometimes, mother would turn into a maniac when it came to cleaning. She kept cleaning late into the evening, even after the maid had left.

Life was repetitive, the same monotonous days and nights. Angad knew that his mother was worried that he had no career. Like any other parent, she too wanted to see her son employed gainfully. However, Angad was clueless about his future. He felt as if nothing was required to survive. The indefiniteness and impermanence created a sense of loss.

His mother had nurtured dreams for him. She used every opportunity to make her point indirectly, but career was the last thing on his mind. "What is a career? Is a good job a sign of success?" Angad was sick of how people treated him for being jobless.

"Why does society judge a person on the basis of his/her career?" Angad had no answers. However, he was clear on applying for a job, at least to keep his mother happy.

Months passed without any progress. Satish uncle grew ill. Angad and his mother visited him several times. He had no physical issues. However, he started losing his memory. It was scary to talk to him. He spoke irrelevant things about *karma*. He talked about his misdeeds as a young man in the services, narrating every incident to his inconsolable wife.

Uncle was developing dementia. He defecated in his bedroom corner and complained about not having a water tap there to clean himself. But he was regular with his trips to the farm, speaking to people along the way, teaching them low-budget farming, intercropping, and above all, keeping an account of everything – a regular statement on living or agriculture. Sometimes, he concluded life is a pendulum, moving both ways to maintain a balance.

He continued his discourse with Angad whenever they visited him. Angad vividly remembered the evening before he passed away. Unlike with the others, his uncle spoke to Angad at length. He talked so much yet was very precise. Perhaps, he knew there would be no tomorrow, at least not for him.

Uncle believed everyone was a puppet at the hands of an evolved chemistry, always under its influence. Urge, desire, longing, attraction to the opposite sex, and so forth were all due to that evolution. Evolution is the real God.

Uncle was a fanatic. He constantly reminded Angad about the number of days left for him to live. Angad was terrified when he found out that his uncle had two glass jars in his private room. He estimated his death and stored stones in one of the pots. He picked one every day and dropped it into the other one. The depleting number in the first bottle reminded him of his remaining days.

It was weird for Angad to see what his uncle did. He, too, quickly counted the days left in his own life, considering a general life span. This disturbed him to no end. He looked inward, thinking that if we are immersed in the present, everything else will be forgotten.

A few days after his uncle's death, Angad entered his room. He wanted to check the jars of stones and was surprised to see that one was empty. Did uncle attract his death by sheer will? It meant he had known it the previous evening. He calculated his death, drew it with his projections and thoughts, and it happened.

Angad lived aimlessly after his uncle's passing. He woke up from bed at noon. He had his food only when hungry. He had lost his sense of time. He accepted almost everything that came his way. He laughed at the idea of having a purpose in life. "Life is only a process; a process of the universe; a method of nature. We, individuals, have no roles to play. The universe is created by all of us through our constant thoughts unintentionally. We can drive the universe as we want to;" such erratic thoughts flooded his mind. We are nothing but our minds. And our mind is in complete control of our surroundings. Our minds act according to what nature dictates.

He wanted to wipe out all emotional feelings in order to set himself emotionally free. He tried to visualise people as simple objects without attaching sentiments to them. In the process, he forgot to laugh, smile or sob. Angad was transforming. He did not want to be affected by simple life events. He looked at people as sufferers of the changing chemistry of the universe, acting as just pawns in the game. Silently, he laughed at them while being one of them.

Angad's mother was worried about his prolonged silence. She wanted him to take up a job. She was too sick and tired of motivating her listless son. She gave up on her positive theories. After the initial setback of her husband's death, Meenakshi had done everything on her own.

She had travelled alone to the city to be with Angad just with the help of an address. She had paid the property taxes and finished all the bank formalities to receive her husband's pension. She had brought out the leader in her courageously. But now, life became so monotonous that she hardly found anything exciting. She believed only Angad could bring some change into her life.

Both mother and son lived with each other's thoughts. They loved each other and did everything to please one another, but she grew worried at her son's blank face, and his inactivity bothered her no end.

Amma spent her time with a few close friends. She renewed her passion for cooking. She would often get caught up on the internet to try out a new recipe. The occasional experiment now became a daily feat, with this the kitchen was turning into a laboratory for her experiments. New and unheard food ingredients were delivered through Amazon. She was trying to not let the monotony creep into her life.

Angad did not express any keenness on his mother's newly acquired culinary skills. However, she prepared unique meals, placed them before Angad, and looked at him for comments. Sometimes, Angad would not notice that he had just been served an experimental dish doled out by his mother. She would lose her patience and grumble at him.

Angad stayed confined to his room. His mother wished to see him employed, married and settled down so that she could enjoy her time with her grandchildren. She felt that something haunted Angad. His total loss of interest in anything was alarming.

One evening, while seated on the veranda, she called out to Angad and asked him to sit next to her. As she sipped her favourite tea, she asked him about his plans, something she had never asked him directly. Not that she did not have the courage, but she did not want to hurt him in any way.

Angad had no answers. All he sought was to be free from the clutches of emotions. His mother continued to talk about a well-structured plan. She was also successful in getting some responses out of Angad at times.

For several months now, Angad had been practising to be non-reactive to the world outside, to create an emotionless mind. He had been trying hard to free himself from this vicious cycle. Many had influenced him, starting from his father, the farmer's family, people around him and those who lived on the Hospital Street.

She could not bear his silence or indifference. She controlled her emotions and waited for Angad to respond positively. Angad spoke very little and was disinterested in anything around. Meenakshi observed his son's strange behaviour all the time. She even contemplated taking her son for treatment but was too anxious about the outcome.

However, Angad knew he was perfectly alright. He believed all those running around him were trying to achieve something trivial and temporary. He believed that we create a temporary world through our thoughts, and we are constantly worrying about this temporary state.

"We are constantly worrying about creating a lot of things that we think would bring us peace. However, worrying about building that peace itself takes away that sense of peace. Why just us? Everything on the earth is trying to make a living. We build homes of brick and mortar. Ants build it with soil; birds with twigs. Is every living being thinking the same way?" Angad caressed his, by-now, thick beard.

At the dining table, Angad expressed his desire to return to Raghu's flat. He was missing his life on the Hospital Street – the men, women and the numerous creatures that flocked to his balcony. He tried to convince his mother without mentioning the possibility of taking up a job.

Meenakshi cried, trying to hide the tears flowing down. She did not say a word. That night, before retiring to her room, she went to Angad's room. Her eyes welled up. The door was open. Standing there, she said, "If you don't care for me, you can go. You have changed a lot recently. I don't know what happened to you. You don't tell me anything! I am concerned about your sudden withdrawal from everything and everyone." Angad smiled and all he could say was: "Good night, *Amma.*" Angad was concerned about his lack of focus. He enjoyed his loneliness. He believed in God. Every moment he wondered about his temporary existence, he viewed his surroundings as if they were new, unique and impermanent.

The television in the living room was showing an unending political debate. The host and the participants were screaming, senselessly speaking on issues that Angad was not interested in because of his state of mind. Meenakshi left the room to turn off the television. But on reaching the living room, she shouted and called for Angad. A ticker ran at the bottom of the screen announcing another mass suicide by an agricultural family. Any such news was heart-wrenching for Angad and his mother.

He collapsed onto the sofa. He recollected the unbearable incident in his life some years ago. Angad's eyes welled up. Meenakshi attributed the reason for Angad's withdrawal to the farmer's family suicide. "Maybe it still haunts him," she thought. The sad story of Narendra and his family seemed to pursue him, day in and day out.

He looked at his mother. She was waiting to hear his reaction to the telecast. However, he did not comment. Instead, his thoughts ran wildly. Looking at her, he started thinking about how he would lose his mother one day. He could not come to terms with the idea of losing her; he could not come to the concept of the quintessential constant change. He needed everything to be still, peaceful and forever. Turning off the television, he went into his room, closed the door and tried to focus on the flowers in a painting hanging on the wall, but failed miserably. He tried to change his focus on a brass lamp on the table but was unable to focus. He then buried his face in the pillow. The fresh fragrance triggered some positivity in him. For a few moments, he gained peace before diving into the abyss of vacuum.

Beams of sunlight poured in through the window, lighting up the room. Angad woke up with a void in his mind. Before his morning routine, he went to the kitchen to check on his mother's well-being. She was busy as usual. She would have planned for breakfast, lunch, evening snacks and a proper dinner too; different dishes for different meals.

Women scheduled their days so well and executed them flawlessly every day. They are outstanding managers. Angad joined his mother in the living room over coffee. The aroma of freshly brewed coffee from her own land gave a heartwarming whiff. "How an aroma stirs the soul?" thought Angad.

Angad turned on the television. Most news channels carried the news of the mass suicides of farmers in Nashik. Every television channel had a different version; some criticised the establishment, while some gently justified the government. They all savoured the new developments before moving on from what they had reported initially. No one addressed the issue. Everyone blamed one another. "Why do these farmers commit suicide?" Meenakshi asked her son cautiously as she did not want to provoke him.

Angad was sad as no one addressed the real issue. He wanted to get on top of his house and shout to tell the world that farmers need to be entrepreneurs, and they should run their farms like a factory and not as a routine chore.

Meenakshi continued talking about soaring prices in the cities while the farmers who toiled hard for the produce were handed out just half of that. She adjusted her voice, gathered her courage, and asked Angad, "Do you have any update about that family?" Angad was thinking about them just then, so he was not surprised that she asked.

"No, *Amma*! But I always think about them, and I still don't sleep many nights thinking about them. I feel guilty. I too had a role in that tragic case."

"You did it for your bank. How could you have been a cause for their unhappy ending?" replied his mother.

"I don't know. We can justify saying all that. But I am deeply hurt for having been a part of that bank. All these years, I wished that one day I would see the farmer and his family happy and abundant. I would imagine them as a wealthy family."

Angad was convinced that the family could have done better. They had a strong, dedicated team of labourers and other resources. Like he had done a thousand times, Angad once again painted a picture of Mrs. Narendra Prasad and saw the grown-up girls, who had escaped the jaws of death, running around their house happily, just like in the past. He saw abundance in and around their home—heaps of grain, parked tractors and a prosperous farm.

A farmer essentially must be a businessman first. Only those who can handle money wisely can become successful businessmen. The wise will never disrespect money. They will not require subsidies or freebies. Farmers must be taught to balance income and expenditure.

Angad lectured his mother on farming, at least from what he understood through observing Narendra Prasad and his uncle Satish. His mother was in awe of her son's business sense. She was happy that he was vocal. He continued to talk about business. Only a natural calamity could destroy farming. Otherwise, farmers are strong and bold enough to run their businesses. Most farmers consider farming to be a ritual. A farmer must adhere to a proper schedule. Every action must be charted. Angad tutored his mother and insisted that she listen to him. He did not let her leave even as it began to get dark. His mother was ecstatic that after a long time, Angad was vocal again. She felt it was a big change.

A few birds on the parapet chirped continuously as if applauding what Angad had said. Mother finally got up to light the evening lamp. Angad kept rambling on without anyone to listen to him. He looked onto the road where a few people were walking. He thought about millions of farmers who feed the country but did not gain anything in return. Were they ill-fated? Was it *karma*?

His mother returned to the veranda with a lit brass lamp. The smell of burnt oil mixed with incense enveloped the porch giving it a divine feel. She evoked the five elements guiding the lamp all around her, repeating "*deepam, deepam....*" She then placed it reverently amongst pictures of Hindu gods, and a smiling portrait of her late husband, with yellow vermilion on his forehead. This daily ritual lasted several minutes before she switched on all the lights. She turned to Angad and said, "Why don't you go and check on that family once?"

Angad had thought many a time about the possibility but hadn't dared to visit the village. It could invite the wrath of the people around. Most of them in the hamlet had known him as a recovery officer.

"Can you come with me? I don't know how the

local people will react on seeing me. I have no idea about the family. I know that only Prasad died while his wife and daughters survived. My God! I don't think I can face them." Angad could not even think of meeting them.

"Me? For what? How will that help? To safeguard you?" she smiled. "No problem. I'll come with you. My grown-up son needs my protection!" she laughed.

CHAPTER FOURTEEN

Next Saturday, the team of the mother and son, set out for a long ride – back to the village that he had always loved.

His mother had covered her head with her *pallu*. Nearly one and a half hours of a smooth drive had brought them back to the countryside. A lot had changed in the few years that he had sieved through. The greenery had vanished and many buildings had come up, taking the place of the small shops that were previously there. It did not take too long to reach Narendra Prasad's house. Angad's heart was thumping. He was not sure if the bank had acquired the house and was reluctant to enter. So, he asked his mother to check. His mother held his hand and pulled him inside. "Follow me," she said and stepped on the porch.

The exterior of the house looked more or less the same. Rusted tractors and tillers were still around. The smell of cow dung and hay filled the air. Cattle were tethered to stakes and hens intermittently clucked.

"Anyone there?" *Amma* boldly asked.

There was no response. But after a few minutes, Narendra Prasad's wife showed up. She looked the same; there was not much change in her appearance, apart from a few stray strands of grey which made her look graceful. She was surprised to see Angad and an older woman. She cried on seeing them but wiped her tears with the end of her saree and invited them inside.

A long story followed, amidst serving tea and snacks. Mrs. Prasad had no resentment towards Angad. She revealed that only Narendra Prasad had died while the three of them had miraculously escaped death to start life anew. She also felt that what Angad did was a part of his duty, and he had never harassed the family for repayment.

Narendra Prasad's wife had mentioned that her children would return home by five O'clock. The three had managed to balance farm work and studies. The lady sobbed off and on and was consoled by Angad's mother; she continued to praise her daughters for managing the farms.

It was past noon. Angad wanted to return home, but the lady insisted on preparing lunch for them. Angad's mother helped her in the preparation of food. Both of them were widows, they had found something in common between them.

Angad was keen to know about the loan and the acquisition, but he dared not to ask. However, the lady mentioned that they suffered a lot financially. The bank attachment was put on hold after the deadline due to the police case on charges of abetment to suicide by the bank. The little money that Angad paid on their behalf had also helped.

"We want to return your money," Mrs. Prasad said. With no one to help the following season, they farmed without borrowing a single penny. "My daughters lost their teenage years to farming but now the loan has almost been paid," the lady said through her tears. Angad interrupted to mention that his visit was not to seek the money he paid on their behalf and asked: "But how did you manage that? Your daughters have been more than sons," he exclaimed, pleasantly surprised.

Amma and Mrs. Narendra Prasad sat next to each together, lost in the conversation. They both spoke as if they had known each other for decades.

For Mrs. Narendra Prasad, life had come to a standstill. Many relatives would have shown up, but for the financial troubles, they faced. It was the loyal labourers who did not stop working on the farm. They wept quietly at the loss of a kind-hearted landlord. Of course, they did not know that their landlord was in debt and it was slowly consuming him. A few of them even approached Mrs. Narendra Prasad's family to offer whatever little financial support they could. They were loyal to the family of their genial landlord, as he had always cared for them.

In distress, Mrs. Narendra Prasad could not care much for the land but the labourers did not stop working. They showed moral courage and took the lead by continuing to work in the fields. They lacked guidance, for which they turned towards the girls, who helped them in some way or the other. Often the girls broke down while thinking of their doting father, though it made them stronger and hard-headed. The girls decided to settle their father's debt and the workers decided to join them in achieving their goals by offering their unconditional support. However, they were sceptical about achieving the goals.

The young minds took to the internet to check agricultural patterns, input expenditures, intercropping and saleability. Agriculture officer, Siddique was an encyclopaedia who supported the budding entrepreneurs at every critical stage of the crops. They ensured that the entire length and breadth of the land was put to good use.

The police visited their home often. They enquired if the bank officials were harassing them. Some senior bank officials also called on, but the family was unsure why they had come. Meanwhile, the girls sought time from the bank to repay the loan, and they repaid everything they made from farming to the bank. All that was missing was the towering presence of the iconic Narendra Prasad. Apart from that, things were definitely getting better.

Working on a shoestring budget, the girls worked without anyone's help. Initially, no one took them seriously. Even the workers had their doubts. However, after eight long months, they got a bumper harvest. With minimum expenditure, the price from yield was optimum; the girls used non-traditional buyers for their produce. Tears of happiness rolled down the cheeks of the labourers. They repaid nearly twenty-five thousand to the bank, making significant progress. The bankers were more than happy that the loan was being settled despite the case being status quo as ordered by the court.

When one decides to do something sincerely, nature supports them. Almost every day, the girls went off to their fields in the morning. They talked about a never-before bumper harvest that attracted buyers from the nearby cities to pay in advance for an abundant crop. Cultivation was based on demand, and they looked for future buyers immediately after sowing. They could always get a higher price from their buyers, be it a pizza chain or an online grocery store in the city.

As Mrs. Narendra Prasad finished narrating her story, the girls appeared. They looked tired and worn out after the day-long classes. They still stood in the foyer upon seeing Angad, a bit nervous and perhaps doubtful about his visit.

Angad's mother broke the silence by saying, "Your mother is very proud of you." They continued to stand there without giving any reaction. Their posture and eyes displayed maturity, way beyond their age.

Meenakshi's face glowed. She showed interest in the girls. She checked out the elder daughter from top to bottom, inspecting her. Meenakshi asked them several questions – name, age, course, college, interests, and many others in a breath. Angad was feeling embarrassed. He thought it was inappropriate to interview the girls this way. It sounded more like bullying. But they politely and most diplomatically replied to her queries. They were no longer the same children who used to play jumping over heaps of dry hay. They had turned from young girls to beautiful women in a short span!

The questions did not bother them until Meenakshi turned to Mrs. Narendra Prasad and pointing at the elder one, said; "I think it is time to look for a groom."

The girl did not blush. She stood there asking her mother's permission to leave while Mrs. Narendra Prasad made some casual comments. Angad's mother, lost in her dreams, continued to smile, looking at the girls. Angad was relieved after hearing how the family had survived their ordeal. The guilt that was dangling in the air had finally lifted.

He suggested that they should leave as it would take a long ride to reach home. Meenakshi agreed and stood up to leave. As Angad walked towards his bike, *Amma* whispered something in Mrs. Narendra Prasad's ear. They kept talking in a serious tone. They exchanged phone numbers. The way they talked and giggled; it seemed like they had been friends for a long time. They hugged each other, *Amma* was reluctant to leave. If Mrs. Narendra Prasad had invited her to stay over, she would have agreed to spend a night.

Angad kick-started the two-wheeler and signalled his mother to sit pillion. She waved until Mrs. Narendra Prasad was not visible anymore. "*Amma*, it's a bit late. I hope we reach home before it turns dark." She wasn't listening to what Angad said to her. Instead, she kept praising the girls. Meenakshi worked on her desire to make the elder girl her daughter-in-law, to bring her home decked up in the bright bridal dress.

Angad set his eyes on the road, watching the tyre measure every foot of the way. His mind continued to be farming in the fields in the hope of a bountiful harvest for tomorrow.